Ans	_____	M.L.	_____
ASH	_____	MLW	_____
Bev	_____	Mt.Pl	_____
C.C.	_____	Nl.M	_____
C.P.	_____	Ott	_____
Dick	6/08	PC	_____
DRZ	_____	PH	_____
ECH	3/10	P.P.	8/07
ECS	_____	Pion.P.	11/06
Gar	_____	Q.A.	2/08
GRM	1/07 Allen	Riv	_____
GSP	_____	RPP	_____
G.V.	_____	Ross	6/07 (Lydia)
Har	_____	S.C.	11/07 (Jant)
JPCP	_____	St.A.	_____
KEN	_____	St.J	_____
K.L.	_____	St.Joa	_____
K.M.	_____	St.M.	_____
L.H.	_____	Sgt	7/06 (McSpa)
LO	_____	T.H.	_____
Lyn	_____	TLLO	_____
L.V.	1/09	T.M.	_____
McC	_____	T.T.	_____
McG	_____	Ven	_____
McQ	5/06 Suter	Vets	_____
MIL	_____	VP	_____
JUB.	10/08 (Altani)	Wat	2/06
	MBull 6/09	Wed	_____
		WIL	_____
		W.L.	_____

STOLEN SECRET

On hearing an intruder downstairs, Lisa Clive's worst fears are realised — a valuable portrait by her late father, Carlton Clive, is missing. To prevent her mother discovering the theft, Lisa determines to recover the painting herself, enlisting the aid of family friend Philip Parker and also mysterious newcomer, Mark. As Lisa begins to feel a reluctant attraction for Mark, an unwelcome family secret is revealed. But who will finally steal her heart — and who can she trust?

ANNE HEWLAND

STOLEN SECRET

Complete and Unabridged

LINFORD
Leicester

First published in Great Britain in 2005

First Linford Edition
published 2005

British Library CIP Data

Hewland, Anne
    Stolen secret.—Large print ed.—
Linford romance library
1. Love stories
2. Large type books
I. Title
823.9′2 [F]

ISBN 1–84617–068–0

Published by
F. A. Thorpe (Publishing)
Anstey, Leicestershire

Set by Words & Graphics Ltd.
Anstey, Leicestershire
Printed and bound in Great Britain by
T. J. International Ltd., Padstow, Cornwall

This book is printed on acid-free paper

1

'That's so unfair.' Carol Clive was frowning. 'Breaking into your holiday like this.'

Lisa put her mobile phone back into her bag, smiling ruefully at her mother.

'I did tell them to let me know if there were any problems. It's just unfortunate that something's come up.'

It had been essential to take her mother away for this spring break, even though Lisa had known they were busy at work.

Her mother smiled back.

'Oh, well. Can't be helped I suppose, and we've enjoyed the greater part of the week without anyone hassling you.'

They were walking along the promenade at Llandudno with a fresh breeze from the sea ruffling their hair, and the sun in their faces and with Bobby, Carol's beloved cairn terrier, trotting along beside them.

Yes, Lisa thought, this break had been a good idea. Just what her mother needed. Carol Clive hadn't said anything, she wouldn't, but it had been this week, ten years ago, when Lisa's father had died.

Carlton Clive was the much-acclaimed, larger-than-life landscape and portrait artist. But the hurdle of the anniversary was now safely past, several days ago.

Lisa said, 'If I drive back today, I can stay the night and be with you again tomorrow.'

'Oh, no. I won't have you driving there and back. Bobby and I will come with you.' But Carol was looking disappointed. Reflecting her mood, Bobby whined softly.

'Nonsense. I enjoy driving and it isn't that far. You stay, if you're sure you'll be all right on your own.'

Carol Clive laughed and said, 'I'm on first-name terms with everyone in the hotel and you know it. That excursion is booked for tomorrow. I can sit with the Coopers and I'll be fine. And we can hardly disappoint Janice when she's looking forward to having Bobby for the day, can we?'

Lisa laughed back. She had certainly struck gold when she had chosen the hotel on the strength of its dogs-welcome policy.

'That's true. So that's settled and I'll be back in no time.'

Carol was frowning again.

'Will you be all right in the house on your own?'

'Mother, I shall be fine,' Lisa said patiently. 'We have a perfectly good alarm system.'

She drove off within half an hour, still smiling. Secretly she was pleased that things had turned out this way. She hadn't engineered it on purpose, of course not, she would never deliberately disrupt her mother's holiday but this way, she would have a night at home on her own — the perfect opportunity.

For some time now, Lisa had been

planning to go through her father's old sketchbooks and papers in his attic studio to collect material for a book about his life. A fitting memorial for a wonderful man and a much-needed source of income.

Carlton Clive had left them with a mountain of debts and even selling off most of his paintings hadn't got them out of the situation altogether. But when she had tried to hint, tactfully, at doing something of the sort, Carol Clive seemed reluctant even to discuss it. Lisa couldn't understand it. But this was probably the best way. If she could make a start and show her mother how well the project was coming along, she was certain that Carol would be won over.

What was that? Lisa's head shot up from the desk. What time was it? She hadn't intended going to sleep but somehow she had slumped down on to her notes. Above her the attic skylight was black. Brushing the curls off her eyes, she looked at her watch. Half past two. She frowned into the silence, every sense alert. Nothing.

Lisa just couldn't understand why her mother seemed so averse to this idea, because the papers in the attic studio contained no worrying personal details. They were mostly sketchbooks and her father's newspaper cuttings about his exhibitions, and a pile of photographs, pushed together haphazardly along with publicity shots of Carlton Clive and his work.

She paused. Yes, that was strange. Lisa frowned at the framed photo of her mother and father on their honeymoon. Why was that here? It belonged on her mother's bedside table. Lisa wondered when Carol had moved it.

She picked it up. Her parents looked so young and happy, her father a commanding presence as always, his beard greying a little even then, his flamboyant charm leaping out of the photo with the handsome smile, and her mother neat and precise with the short fair hair and the blue eyes that

5

echoed Lisa's own.

Her father had been such an amazing person and he and Carol had been such a wonderful couple, so happy together.

Lisa sighed. Perhaps her mother was still grieving secretly, even ten years on, and could no longer bear to look at her younger carefree self.

If so, Lisa's secret project might not be such a good idea. A pity because the material she had uncovered this evening would be invaluable for the book. But there again, she smiled as a more cheerful thought struck her. If her mother was deeply unhappy, assisting with Lisa's book might help. A kind of therapy? If only Lisa could persuade her of that.

Lisa leaped up. No, she hadn't imagined it. It was there again — a muffled crash from downstairs. The hairs on the back of her neck were tingling. There was someone down there.

Lisa didn't stop to think. She snatched up one of her father's old walking sticks and made for the stairs, her heels clumping noisily on the bare wood. Making a lot of noise was recommended in such situations, wasn't it? She switched the lights on as she went, clattering the stick against the banister rail.

'Hey!' she shouted.

It was working. Already there were sounds of panic-stricken flight from the ground floor, and now she was passing the burglar alarm switch on the middle landing. She should have thought of that before. She pressed it swiftly and the alarm shrieked out into the darkness beyond the front door, which was standing open. A flash of someone in black threw themselves outside, into blinding light as the security beam activated.

Why hadn't that happened earlier? No time to worry about it now. She stopped at the door, peering out beyond the light to the shrubs in the hillside garden and the stone wall and steeply cobbled lane beyond. Get hold of the police, she thought.

She looked around the hall. No sign of any mess or hurried ransacking. Oh, no! Whatever was she thinking of? What about the painting? Her mother's most precious possession. Carol Clive had parted with all the others with grim determination, selling them off to pay those crippling debts. But not that one. Never *Gemini*.

Lisa's head was pounding as she hurried into the sitting-room. And yes, the deep crimson of the wall over the fireplace was empty. A lone streak of dust marked the space.

2

Lisa's stomach lurched in despair. Forgetting all caution, she turned and ran out on to the drive. Had that dark figure been carrying anything? She couldn't remember but he must have been.

'Are you OK?' There was a voice calling from the gate.

Lisa jumped, suspicious now of anyone and anything, and that was silly because the thief wouldn't be hanging around. Besides, this man, although tall and dark-haired, was wearing a silver-grey jacket. Far too conspicuous. She called back, 'We've been burgled. Just now. I actually saw him.'

'Which way did he go?' A warm, strong voice, a voice you could trust.

She pointed towards the road and said, 'But he'll be well away by now.'

'Worth a try. Go in and lock the

door. I'll get him.'

He was off before she could protest.

For all they knew, the thief might double back during the pursuit and help himself to everything else worth having, not that there was much left of any value nowadays.

Anyway, she had better call the police and the sooner, the better. She hesitated. Once she'd done that, the next step would be inevitable. Her mother would have to know. And you never know, at any moment, the helpful stranger might be back, with the painting in one hand and the robber clutched firmly in the other.

She sighed regretfully. No, that would be impossible. He wouldn't be able to manage both at once. But forget the robber, if he'd retrieved the painting that would be enough.

Besides, she'd better have a quick look round to see where the thief had got in. So far, she only knew where he'd got out, through the front door. If one of the ground floor windows had been forced, she needed to do something about it, although the police would want to look at it.

Although the house was detached, with steeply-sloping gardens on all sides and an imposing drive, outside appearances were deceptive. It was not large inside and Lisa had whipped round the ground floor windows and checked the back door in minutes. Nothing. She was still frowning about that when the doorbell rang.

Yes, her Good Samaritan, back already. That was great. She flung open the door, smiling a question and her face fell.

His arms were wide in apology.

'I'm sorry. There wasn't a sign of him.'

Lisa fought to hide her disappointment. Now her mother would have to know and Lisa didn't want to think about how Carol would feel, or what she would say. But that wasn't his fault and it had been kind of him to make the effort. She said, 'Thanks anyway. It was good of you to try.' Yes, he looked kind, brown eyes and smile lines at the sides of his mouth.

'When I got out on to the main road, I could hear a car setting off at speed. I'd hoped I might get a glimpse of the make or the colour at least. Something to tell the police.' He shrugged his shoulders. 'I just wasn't fast enough. And that might have been somebody who was just driving past. But the streets are pretty deserted out there.'

'It sounds likely that it was him. I'm sure he had this planned and knew what he was doing. And if there was no-one else around . . . ' Lisa stopped abruptly. What on earth was this man doing, wandering about at this time of night? She said abruptly, 'So where were you going? I haven't seen you around here before.' Too abrupt, as her mother was always telling her.

'Oh, I don't live too far away. And you walk for miles, don't you, with a dog?'

'Yes, I suppose you would.' Lisa

looked round. 'But where is it?'

He looked round, too, flipping a hand to dark, tousled hair.

'Oh, no. Must have run off. I'll have to go. Sorry.' He was already backing away, ready to run. 'You've called the police?'

'No. Not yet.' She had a sudden urge to run her hands through the wilderness of his hair and felt herself blushing. What on earth was she thinking of? And at a time of crisis, too. But of course, that explained it. All her emotions would be heightened and in inappropriate ways. Lucky that he couldn't read her thoughts.

'Call them,' he was saying. 'You can tell them about the car if you like. Sorry I didn't get the make. Sorry I couldn't be more help.'

'That's OK.' Suddenly she wasn't sure about him. He seemed angry; she could sense it. But why? Because the thief had got away? He was half out of the gate now, waving and turning back to shout, 'Call the police. Straightaway.'

'I will. Hey,' she cried as he flashed away out of sight. 'I don't know your name.' The police would be sure to ask. They would want a statement from him. She sighed because she would have liked to know his name, too. But perhaps when he'd found his dog, he would come back. Surely he would.

He didn't come back. He hadn't even turned up by the time the police arrived the following morning. They were working at full capacity, someone had told her, because there were several accidents on the motorway and asked if she could make the house secure without too much trouble.

'Yes, I can. I told you there's no sign of a forced entry.' The voice on the phone had advised her to set her alarm and have a good night's sleep.

There wasn't much chance of that, not when she couldn't imagine how the thief had got in. The words kept going round in her head. No sign of a forced entry. The police weren't going to be too impressed by that.

They were not. Two young men took details as rapidly as possible to enable them to fill in their forms and making it obvious they didn't feel there was much chance of achieving any kind of result. Their major duty seemed to be in giving her a crime number for insurance purposes. But there were raised eyebrows for the story of the mysterious stranger who had forgotten to give his name.

'Now, Miss Clive,' Detective Constable Wethers said, 'let me run through this again. You were alone in the house working on the top floor and you hadn't set the alarm?'

'I wouldn't, would I? I only set it when I go to bed. Obviously.'

She didn't want to seem rude but he was rattling her.

'But you said you were asleep.'

'I didn't intend going to sleep. I was busy. I had a lot to do.'

And you're not the only people in a hurry, she thought crossly. With all these distractions I'm nowhere near doing as much as I'd intended.

'So you know you didn't set the security alarm. Perhaps also you didn't secure the front door?'

'What? But I'm sure I did. I must have done. I always do.' Lisa huffed out a breath of frustration. She couldn't actually remember. Such a simple act, which she had performed so many times before without thinking about it.

Unfortunately the evidence that she couldn't have locked the door was staring them in the face: no sign of any forced entry, the door standing wide open. No doubt she'd destroyed valuable fingerprint evidence in shutting it for the rest of the night.

The policeman nodded but she didn't like the way they were biting their lips. They didn't believe a word of it.

'Perhaps on this occasion, you simply forgot? It's easily done.'

'I'm as sure as I can be that I didn't forget, without actually remembering.'

'Yes, I see,' D C Wethers said. 'Now,

can you tell us a bit more about this member of the public you mentioned?'

Lisa was almost wishing that they would return to hasty form-filling mode. Why didn't they seem to be glossing over all the bits that mattered and concentrating on the unfortunate parts that didn't? They were trying to be polite but they were conveying scepticism and disapproval in several small and subtle ways — a slight sideways movement of the head or half turning to look at each other, particularly in the shakiest bits.

She could hardly blame them. The stranger had appeared out of the blue, or out of the darkness, seemingly eager to help. But at half past two in the morning? And difficult to explain why she had trusted him straightaway. She was beginning to wonder about that herself.

She stuck to emphasising the silver-grey jacket when she had been certain the thief in the hallway had been dressed entirely in black. So, of course, silver-jacket man was OK from that fact alone and she was surprised the police didn't seem convinced.

★ ★ ★

Lisa still wasn't sure how to tackle her mother, although she would be driving back later that afternoon to share the last night of their spring break before bringing Carol Clive home the following morning.

Should she phone her to tell her about the theft, to lessen the shock? Or would it make things worse?

No, far better to break the news in person. And, no, Lisa told herself sternly, this did not mean that she was putting it off. Besides, her mother was going off on that coach trip they'd booked, wasn't she?

Lisa was wishing by now she had never stolen that one night to start going through her father's posthumous notes and papers. It would take longer than she'd expected, she'd realised that much. Even without the unfortunate events of the night.

She sighed, unwilling to let go of her precious fantasy of presenting her mother with the outline of the proposed book on her return.

'You see?' Lisa had imagined herself saying, 'Nothing here to worry about at all. And it would be the answer to all our financial problems. And we won't have to ask Philip to sell the last painting for us.'

Lisa slumped down on to the desk. She'd better make a start at tidying the evidence away, she supposed. Couldn't be giving her mother too many unwelcome surprises all at once. What she already had in store for her was bad enough. Would the insurance company pay out?

That might help their financial situation, except that she wasn't convinced they would be willing to pay when everyone seemed so certain Lisa had left the front door unlocked. She hadn't thought of that. This whole thing was getting worse and worse.

The cordless phone rang and Lisa almost leaped off her chair. It had to be the police. They must have found the painting. Thank goodness for that.

'Hello?' she cried happily.

'Hello, dear. You sound chirpy this morning.'

Lisa swallowed, endeavouring to rediscover a suitable element of chirpiness.

'You'll never guess what's happened,' her mother was saying.

'Oh? Won't I?' And neither will you, Lisa thought unhappily.

'And I'm so glad I caught you before you set off, because after you left, yesterday afternoon, I bumped into Jenny Palmerston. You remember?'

Lisa shook her head but that wouldn't matter because her mother would ramble on about Jenny Palmerston for several minutes now, giving Lisa a chance to pull herself together. And, yes, she did remember Mum mentioning her, now she thought about it. She was an old school friend.

'And the upshot is she's actually living just outside the town, a beautiful house, you've no idea. She was so disappointed she hadn't known sooner that we would be staying in North Wales.'

Take deep breaths, Lisa thought. She had no idea where this tale was going and didn't much care. No, she would have to tell her, as soon as her mother paused for breath. It wasn't fair to put it off one minute longer.

'So I really do hope you won't mind.' Her mother sounded wheedling, doubtful and apologetic. All at once. Although not very apologetic.

'Sorry? Won't mind what?'

'Oh, do try and concentrate, dear. Jenny Palmerston has asked me to have a week with her and this means you won't have to rush back for me. All that driving, I wasn't happy about that in the first place. I know there's no point in asking if you'd like to come and stay with Jenny, too, although of course the invite extends to you.

'I knew you'd be itching to get back to work. But if you came for me next weekend, you could have a night here and meet Jenny, and it would make up for cutting your holiday short.'

'So it would. But we can arrange that nearer the time,' Lisa said airily, feeling as if a huge cloud had lifted. She had gained a reprieve. She didn't need to tell her mother about the painting today after all. Perhaps not ever because now she had a whole week of extra time. Surely that would be enough for even D C Wethers to get his act together and come up with something?

She frowned, remembering how he had hardly seemed brimful of enthusiasm. Well, if the police didn't make much of an effort, which seemed more than likely, she would have to do something about tracking the painting down herself.

3

A week. A whole seven days to sort things out. Excellent. A week would surely be long enough.

But to do what exactly? The euphoria began to fade. She could badger the police twice a day to see if they'd got anywhere, she supposed. That might keep them on their toes. But somehow she wasn't sure that would be a good idea. An overload of too little man-power, too many crimes and too much paperwork was hardly their fault.

Besides, whatever she did would have to be undercover, wouldn't it? She didn't want to risk the Press getting hold of this, otherwise the whole object would be defeated before Lisa had begun. Good old friend, Jenny, might keep Carol Clive busy with so many delightful outings that they never bothered to switch on the TV news or pick up a newspaper, but you couldn't count on it.

What she needed, Lisa decided, was someone who could be taken on board in an advisory capacity, someone knowledgeable but discreet.

She would have to phone Philip. Lisa hesitated. She should have told him straightaway she supposed, but things were a bit awkward at the moment.

Even before they had gone away, she'd suspected Philip was on the brink of asking her out, moving on from their casual friendship. But she wasn't ready for that. She sighed, not understanding herself. In many ways, Philip would be perfect. She liked him, her mother liked him, he had known her father and had been so helpful in getting good prices for the work they had been forced to sell. And if she could actually marry Philip, their financial worries would be over and they would never need to sell *Gemini*. But that would be ridiculous. She didn't love him. Not yet.

She bit her lip. Selling *Gemini* didn't

come into it now, did it? Telling Philip about the theft would be almost as bad as telling her mother. It was so, so tempting to leave him in the dark as well. But the chances of getting anywhere without his inside knowledge of the art world would be minimal.

Lisa picked up the phone and dialled his number.

'Lisa!' Philip said. Her mother had always remarked on his elegant speaking voice. 'Are you back already? I was going to give you a ring but I wasn't sure whether you'd said morning or afternoon? I would very much like to take you and your delightful mother out for lunch.'

'My mother isn't here yet.' Lisa explained about the problem at work and the old school friend, realising that her explanation was becoming more and more drawn out and that once again, she was putting things off. She paused. 'Philip, I'm afraid I have something to tell you. The painting has been stolen.'

'What?' His voice rose. 'Not *Gemini*? That's terrible. But what about you? Are you all right?'

At least, Lisa thought miserably, he had understood straightaway. There wasn't a hint of outraged disbelief.

'I'm fine.'

'When? What happened? No, second thoughts, don't tell me yet. I'm coming round. Right now.'

'OK,' Lisa said unhappily.

Better if he had allowed her to come out with the whole thing straightaway, she thought, switching off and carrying the phone into the sitting-room. Because you never knew. The police might just call.

Once there, she arranged the chairs so that they were no longer facing the fireplace wall and the empty space. But that looked even more obvious. No, there was no way of making it look better. Perhaps if she took him into the dining-room instead ... even worse because Mum always entertained Philip in the sitting-room and usually with a little glass of something.

You would think Philip was nearer her mother's age, although he couldn't have been more than in his mid-thirties. But he deserved VIP treatment, for coming to their rescue and selling the paintings.

And for good prices, even before they became fashionable and hadn't been that easy to shift. Lisa and Carol wouldn't have known where to start. All except *Gemini*, of course, the last one they had. And no way could her mother be persuaded into parting with that.

Philip kept his word, as he always did, and was round in less than half an hour. Lisa opened the door to him in relief. She should have known that Philip would be a tower of strength, standing there with his usual air of calm detachment, the very quality that made Lisa's mother feel so safe with him.

You wouldn't think there was a crisis on, to look at him. Not a fair hair out of place and the dark pinstriped suit was as neat as always, complemented with a toning shirt and tie.

As she looked more closely, Lisa realised his forehead was damp and that the grey eyes weren't focusing on her. That seemed odd. But obviously he would be upset about the painting; he had always loved it so much. She could hardly blame him.

He had always wanted to sell this one for them so badly, she knew that. He had always said it was the best of the lot. And now she had lost it. She gave a rueful half shrug.

'I'm so sorry.'

He strode past her into the hall.

'This is dreadful. Terrible.'

'Do come in, Philip.'

He hurried into the sitting-room and was immediately straight out again, as if he could hardly bear to look at the empty wall.

'What happened? How did they get in?'

'I was just about to tell you. But don't say anything until I've finished, OK?' Lisa walked over to the fireplace and stood with her back to the wall.

At some stage in the telling, Lisa began to feel irritated with him. He was an art dealer, wasn't he? The painting would never have been his, it would merely have passed through his hands. His reactions were becoming over the top as he clutched his forehead in despair.

She got to the end and stopped, swallowing hard, ready to defend herself. But he looked calmer now.

'So the police think you didn't lock the door?'

Here we go, over and over again. There was no getting away from that one awkward question. Lisa sighed.

'I'm sure I must have done. I can't see how I could have forgotten.' She paused miserably. 'Yes, they do.'

He said abruptly, 'That means you were in danger yourself. That worries me more than the loss of the painting.'

'Does it?' Perhaps she was misjudging him. Perhaps his concern was for her, not *Gemini*. She hadn't thought of that, and she should have done. If her suspicions were right and he was thinking about proposing to her, of course he would be worried about her.

Oh, dear, with dreading the thought of telling him about this catastrophe, she'd pushed Philip's intentions towards herself to the back of her mind. She was almost wishing he hadn't come round. How complicated everything was.

Philip's voice softened.

'You were here on your own with the door unlocked and up on the top floor, no lights visible. The thieves must have thought the house was empty.'

'The thief. I only saw one.'

'Bound to be a gang, I'd have thought. Stealing to order.'

'You think so? The police didn't mention anything like that.'

'When I think of you coming downstairs and disturbing them, anything could have happened.'

'I suppose so. But if he was stealing

to order and was only interested in that painting . . . '

'If you'd disturbed them a minute or so sooner . . . ' Philip was shaking his head. And, yes, he was sweating. It was sweet of him to care about her safety so much, she supposed. 'My dear girl . . . ' At last he was spreading his arms to enfold her.

Lisa relaxed against his chest for a moment. This was what she needed, wasn't it?

He muttered, 'And what about that other man? The one who said he would help?'

'Yes.' Lisa was unable to help smiling. He was the one bright spot in the whole thing, except that he hadn't got back to her yet. Somehow she was unfolding herself from Philip's embrace.

Philip didn't seem to notice. He was pausing dramatically, looking round as if expecting him to walk in at any minute.

'So where is he? Surely the police want him to make a statement?'

Lisa felt an urgent need to stick up for her mystery man.

'I haven't actually seen him since but he may have gone directly to the police station. He was in a hurry. I told you. He'd lost his dog.'

'Yes.' Philip was shaking his head. 'But you didn't see him with a dog?'

'No. He heard the burglar alarm going off and came to see if he could help. I expect the dog ran off then.' She frowned. What had he said? She couldn't recall the exact words. 'I'm not sure whether he said he had a dog or not now. Does it matter?'

'Of course it matters. This strange man could be your thief, or at least one of the gang.'

'He certainly is not the thief.' Lisa felt unexpectedly angry. 'His jacket was the wrong colour.'

'Easy enough to discard a jacket, or put on another one.'

'Why should he? The thief obviously wasn't expecting me to see him. He probably thought the house was empty.

And why bother coming back again? It doesn't make sense.' Her voice tailed off. She was beginning to doubt herself now. Lisa took a deep breath. 'Please, do sit down, Philip. This isn't helping. I need to think what to do next.'

He sat down, straight-backed, staring at her.

'What is there to do? The police are on the case, as they say. And when they find the painting, may I suggest that you advise your mother, and in the strongest terms possible, that she should sell?' He leaned forward a little. 'You see, if you had only sold last year, when we first began discussing the possibility . . . '

'You discussed it. My mother wouldn't entertain the idea.'

He ignored the interruption.

'You wouldn't have had to go through any of this. And when your mother comes back, surely having the painting in the house again would be a constant worry for her after what's happened.' He paused. 'Assuming you get it back. But I'm sure you will.'

'So am I. I have to get it back.'

'How is your mother?' Philip's voice was concerned. 'This must have been a terrible shock for her.'

Lisa could feel her face pulling itself into several different expressions all at once.

'She doesn't know.'

'What? You haven't told her? You have to tell her.'

'I know. I know. But I'm hoping it may be recovered by the time she gets back so I won't need to tell her.' She smiled at him hopefully. 'You do think there's every chance of getting it back, don't you? You must do, if you're still advising us, in the strongest possible terms, to sell.'

Philip's hands were clenching and unclenching on the arms of his chair.

'I meant *if* you get it back, of course. But you can't count on that. In fact, if it was an organised gang, and your meeting with that other man makes that almost certain in my opinion, you may never see it again.'

Lisa was in no mood to have her plans squashed.

'Now you're being defeatist, Philip. I've got an extra week. I explained all that, and I'm going to make use of it. You are the very person to help me.'

He frowned. 'How do you mean?'

She smiled, saying, 'You have so many contacts in the art world. We could go round to everyone you know and ask if *Gemini* has come on to the market. Put out some feelers.'

He was shaking his head already. She might have known. Philip was far too staid and conventional to make any useful contribution.

'I don't think that's a good idea. Why don't you leave the investigation to the police? It's their job.'

'Because I'm not convinced they're going to do anything.'

'I'll tell you what, I can have a word with a friend of mine on the force. He'll get things moving, I can assure you.'

'But we only have a week.' All the

same, for a moment, Lisa was tempted, until something else occurred to her. 'This friend of yours, it wouldn't be D C Wethers, would it? It is, isn't it? I can see it in your face. Philip, he's worse than useless.'

'You can't expect these things to move fast, Lisa. The gang may well have gone to ground, as D C Wethers will have appreciated. I doubt there will be the remotest chance of the painting surfacing yet or being offered for re-sale. And if it's gone to a private collector, that will be the end of it. No, my advice remains the same. Tell Carol as soon as possible and leave this to the police.'

Lisa even managed a smile as she saw him out although she didn't feel like smiling. She had been depending on Philip and he had been no help at all. But she had no intention of sitting back and taking his advice. She would have to act alone, without the benefit of Philip's knowledge and contacts.

There were auction houses and

galleries in Manchester and Leeds, not too far away. And if she made contact by mobile phone, there would be no chance of their knowing who she was.

Concealing her identity was easy; everyone received her courteously, accepting that she was a client eager to purchase a Carlton Clive. But she gained no hint whatsoever where *Gemini* might be.

The various dealers were becoming ever more regretful at having to disappoint her.

'They're very much in demand, I'm afraid. Carlton Clive's works come on to the market so infrequently. We'll certainly see what we can do.'

She made a much-needed cup of coffee and gathered up some of the post that had piled up while they were away. With all the excitement, the daily paperwork had been pushed to one side. And, yes, there was the phone already.

She shot out of the chair, sending the coffee mug flying. This was great, only realising as she reached for the handset that it wouldn't be an early result as the dealers only had her mobile number.

Might be the police though, or even the helpful stranger. Did he have her number? No, unfortunately not. Pull yourself together.

'Hello? Lisa Clive speaking.'

'Oh, hello.' A woman's voice and one Lisa thought she recognised. She couldn't quite place it.

'Pamela Harris here. Is your mother in?'

'I'm afraid not.' Lisa explained about the extended holiday. 'Perhaps I can help.'

'Oh, I don't know. I had hoped to speak to Carol in person.'

'If you could tell me what this is about,' Lisa suggested.

'I'm organising an Antiques Valuation Day in the town hall. Did your mother mention it?'

Had she? Lisa couldn't remember. She certainly didn't recall Carol Clive planning to attend anything like that.

She was beginning to remember who Pamela Harris was and that Carol Clive generally made an effort to avoid her. She was well-meaning but overpowering.

'I sent a short note a few days ago, advising your mother of the change of date. Originally she had to decline, very regretfully, of course, because of the clash with your little break. But we've had a last-minute alteration, a problem with the wiring, very unfortunate considering all the publicity, but the local media have been absolute bricks. And now you're back, this new date will be better for you, won't it? I'm so glad because with Carlton Clive being one of our local heroes, artistically speaking, I didn't want to omit him.'

Note? Lisa shuffled through the pile of post. Where was it? Oh, yes, she wanted to see what she would be letting herself in for before responding one way or the other.

'My father's paintings aren't exactly antiques.'

'No, no. I know that. I didn't mean to offend and goodness, Carol is younger than I am. But the word antique is such a draw in itself. If you find my leaflet, you'll see that. Everything is explained. I was sure Carol would have something of interest for us. Something she could bring along. Something belonging to your father perhaps?'

Lisa felt half-moved and half as if she wanted to giggle. She could just imagine her father puffing himself up about this. Just the kind of thing they had always teased him about.

'We haven't parted with anything like that. We couldn't sell anything of his. We wouldn't want to.' Selling the paintings had been bad enough.

'I do understand. But I want to ensure, in advance, that there will be items of particular interest for our experts to look at. Items of quality.'

Found it. Lisa hitched the phone under her ear and took the leaflet out of the envelope, glancing at the covering letter.

'I thought the idea was that people just turned up to this kind of event, at random, to surprise the experts.'

'Of course they do. We live in hope that there will be surprise items also, but if I relied on that, the event could so easily miss the mark and become dull. And of course, dear, it is for charity.'

'Yes,' Lisa said. She could hardly miss that part and quite right, too, and all credit to Pamela Harris for giving her time and energy to such a good cause. 'I'll see what I can do.' What else could she say? But she wished it hadn't come up just now when she had so much to do and not much time.

Wait a minute. She flicked a finger across her forehead. Experts, Mrs Harris had said. This might prove to be just what she needed, further contacts. This was excellent. She brushed aside the effusive thanks.

'Well, as you said, it is for charity. Of course I'll help.'

There was the added bonus that

when Carol Clive rang that night, Lisa could distract her nicely by asking her advice. Her mother threw herself into the project, albeit at a distance, with enthusiasm.

'I thought we'd avoided Pamela Harris's do but, no, you're quite right. We'll have to trot along with something.'

I, Lisa thought, I shall be doing the trotting, not we. And she could hardly ask her mother to be brief in order to clear the phone network because her mother would want to know who might be calling.

'This will be costing you the earth,' she said at last. 'You should have rung the landline.'

'Oh, yes, you're right. I only intended to stay on a moment, just to make sure everything was fine. Oh, anyway, there's Jenny, I'll have to go. 'Bye.'

Lisa's agreement with Mrs Harris had to be followed up with several calls to discuss the arrangements.

'Naturally, Lisa, I wouldn't expect

you to wait in the queue with everyone else. What we intend is that people like yourself who will be bringing something special will be fast-tracked through, I believe that's the term. And if you arrive before seven you will be whisked through very quickly indeed so your items can be placed on the special display table on the stage. At half past nine, you see, the experts will have worked their way through the queues and can speak to the whole audience about the best finds.'

'I don't mind queuing,' Lisa said. 'I really don't want to be fast-tracked anywhere. Won't it look a bit odd if I get special treatment?'

Mrs Harris said cheerfully she was sure no-one would mind. After all, it was for charity. That useful phrase seemed to mean you could mess people about as much as you liked without anyone objecting.

'I shall try for seven but I have to get home from work and I have other commitments, too. I shall certainly be there but don't worry if you can't whisk me.' The event would surely be more fun from the queue, Lisa thought. And how could she learn anything of use, stuck in a room behind the stage and drinking tea with the favoured few? No, she wanted to be out where the buzz was happening. She wanted to observe the experts.

But having a favoured position might well prove useful later. It could give her a private track-way to the experts if they were to be entertained separately at refreshment time. If they knew nothing themselves they might well provide her with further contacts — and be more willing to share these with her than Philip had been. She would make her request seem innocent, asking how her father's works were selling in the market these days.

Yes, Lisa was feeling pleased she had agreed to go, instead of using her mother's absence as an excuse. Even more so when, by Wednesday, the day of the event, she was beginning to feel decidedly twitchy about the lack of response from her own contacts.

She packed up the items her mother had finally decided upon, a small sketchbook full of doodles, some of her father's brushes, a well-used palette. Even after ten years, handling her father's things brought a sense of grief and she might have wondered at the wisdom of displaying his possessions to the public gaze in this way, if she hadn't been certain her father would have loved it.

Mrs Harris had obviously worked hard to provide her charitable audience with an entertaining evening. There were rows of seats in front of the stage, ready for half-past nine. At the rear of the large hall, there were small tables covered with dark blue cloths where the experts were based, each with a sign so the ticket holders knew which queues to join — China and Glass; Books and Maps; Toys; Miscellaneous; Paintings. Yes, that was where Lisa needed to be. Even with being briefed in advance by

Pamela Harris, she knew which expert would be the most use to her. She even caught a glimpse of D C Wethers in the China and Glass queue.

Although a small queue had formed and was waiting patiently, the table labelled Paintings was empty. Oh, no. Don't say the art expert hadn't turned up and the might have to make do with a hodge-podge opinion from one of the others.

'Where's our expert?' she murmured to the woman waiting in front of her and who was clutching a supermarket carrier bulging with battered frames half-wrapped in yellowing newspaper.

'It's all right,' the woman said. 'He was here a moment ago. He's just discovered something big. You should have been here. It was quite exciting. And now, look, he's taken the young man up on to the stage. They have two security guards there, you see.'

Indeed they had and on loan from the local supermarket by the look of their uniforms. Several figures were

4

Lisa stared at the painting in a mixture of horror and delight. All the sounds in the room merged into one booming noise. She was only aware of herself and *Gemini*, nothing and no-one else but the painting she had worried and cried over and half-dreaded never seeing again, a picture of a young woman in a light dress with a floppy sun-hat hiding her face and hair, sitting quietly, head bent towards the book in her lap as she sat on the grass. Her back was towards the artist as if he had crept up, not wishing to disturb this peaceful sunlit moment in the woodland glade.

Lisa could even see how her father's signature ended fancifully in a flourish to form a trademark butterfly on his work, Gemini with Daisies and Forget-me-Nots.

Lisa looked round frantically, swaying

on her feet. Her fingers were clenched around the box she held and her knuckles were white. Bemused joy was rapidly being overtaken by anger.

'Are you all right, dear?' It was the friendly woman in front of her. 'Do you want to sit down?'

Concerned hands were pressing her towards the expert's empty chair. She had to snap out of this. What must she look like?

'No, I'm fine,' she gasped, while her brain was buzzing swiftly.

She had to think. The painting was safe enough for the moment. It wouldn't be going anywhere for the next few hours; there were too many witnesses. That gave her time to work something out.

What had happened was obvious. She couldn't believe the out and out cheek of the man. Making no attempt to disguise himself because he was even wearing that same jacket. Lisa shook her head. And she had liked him so much and trusted him straightaway.

This proved Philip and the police had been right.

Whom to tell? D C Wethers, obviously. Lisa sighed, knowing how upset Pamela Harris would be, too, when her evening was ruined. Lisa was going to feel awful about that but there was no way she could let it go.

D C Wethers was here to represent officialdom and he was the man to deal with it. She was sure the security guards would assist him if he wanted to make an arrest there and then and undoubtedly, from the audience's point of view, it would add to the excitement of the evening.

The resulting publicity would mean her mother would have to find out, which was a bit of a downside, but as long as they had the painting back, surely that wouldn't matter too much? You never knew, perhaps she would decide to sell after all.

These thoughts and plans had flashed through Lisa's mind in seconds. She flashed them through once more, checking them. Even her mother must agree that this time Lisa wouldn't be rushing into anything, because this plan of action seemed foolproof.

She wondered whether D C Wethers would make his arrest in full view of the audience or take the thief discreetly on one side? Well, that was up to him.

Unfortunately, D C Wethers didn't seem too keen to do either.

'I'll lose my place in the queue.' He squinted up at the stage. 'Are you sure?'

'Of course I'm sure. I'd know my own painting, wouldn't I?'

'Perhaps it's a copy.'

'So why would he bring it here? A copy would have no value. And there are no copies. The original has never left our possession. Not until now.'

D C Wethers sighed. 'All right. No, no.' He shook his head as Lisa made a move to follow him. 'You stay here. This has to be handled appropriately.'

Lisa glared at him, not wanting to be sidelined. 'So when will I get it back? Can I take it home tonight?'

'First things first.' D C Wethers was off, threading his way through Toys and then Books and Maps with a wistful look on his face as he passed the head of the China and Glass queue. It would have looked more appropriate and official if he'd put his own carrier bag down first, Lisa thought.

Lisa stared after him, almost unaware of the crowds around her. Yes, he had got himself on to the stage and was speaking to Mrs Harris. Lisa frowned. Whatever he had said, Mrs Harris didn't seem too worried about it. She was smiling, waving towards the side of the stage. And now D C Wethers was smiling pleasantly, too, and not even flashing his ID badge.

And, yes, the two men were leaving the stage, and going off into the wings. Good, because that meant something was happening. Bad, because Lisa had no way of knowing what it was. She sighed. If it hadn't been for Mrs Harris's feelings, Lisa could have leaped up and denounced him at the dramatic moment when he was laying claim to the painting and telling the expert where he had got it from.

Huh! That would have been interesting. Discovered it in the attic, no doubt, or perhaps he would have claimed that some relatives had picked it up in a junk shop, or bought it at a car-boot sale for fifty pence.

Someone tapped her on the shoulder.

'It's your turn, dear. Are you feeling better? We kept your place.'

Lisa jumped, turning but half-gesturing back towards the stage, where everything appeared peaceful. No, best to carry on as though she knew nothing of what was happening, Besides, Mrs Harris was bearing down on her, with a wide white smile.

'You haven't seen Robert yet? Our expert?'

'I was just about to.' Lisa didn't want to face Mrs Harris. She could feel her face growing red with guilt. However, she allowed herself to be manoeuvred through the process, helped to the chair by her original benefactor who was still convinced she had rushed off because she felt ill.

Concentrate, Lisa thought. Resisting the temptation to turn round and look at the stage, she mumbled something about her father's cherished possessions, knowing she wasn't making a very good effort. Never mind, she would do better later, when it mattered.

'Mrs Harris, I think we have further items of particular interest here,' the expert was saying with a flourish of his luxurious cuff. And here was Mrs Harris, right on cue to guide Lisa to the very place where she most wanted to be, being shown to a seat in the first two rows while Mrs Harris took her parcel, hastily bundling the wrappings into Lisa's cardboard box.

Lisa tried to listen while Mrs Harris explained, again, how the proceedings would run and how at the right moment, Mrs Harris would signal for Lisa to join the party of experts on the stage where their conversation would be milling about up there, including Pamela Harris herself.

What was everyone getting into a huddle about? What had caused all the excitement? Lisa peered over the heads in front of her. They were giving this painting pride of place, whatever it was.

She couldn't see at the moment. Mrs Harris was standing in the way. And that man in the plum-coloured suit with flamboyant sleeves, emerging from his cuffs must be the expert. So who was the owner?

Mrs Harris was saying something to a young man in a silver grey jacket. She moved to one side, revealing the painting.

It was *Gemini*.

relayed by the sophisticated sound system.

'Try and forget that the microphone is there. That's the best way.'

Lisa hardly heard her. From here, the painting was clearly visible and looking so bright and beautiful. But what was happening off stage? What was D C Wethers doing? How long did it take to arrest somebody?

And, yes, here they were. Lisa half rose to her feet. But what was going on? The man in the silver jacket and D C Wethers were shaking hands. The man was coming down the steps and taking a seat farther along the front row, while D C Wethers was scanning the audience. Obviously he would be looking for her.

Lisa scrambled along the row.

'What's happened? Have you told him to report to the station?'

D C Wethers set off down the aisle beside the rows.

'Ah, Miss Clive. No, I'm afraid it was all a misunderstanding. No arrests.

Nothing dramatic whatsoever.'

Lisa chased after him, almost bumping into him as they came to a halt in the Miscellaneous items queue. He actually seemed to be grinning, not taking this seriously at all.

'I don't know what you mean,' Lisa hissed. 'That's our painting. I should know.'

'An understandable mistake but I can assure you it isn't. Mr Ridgely has satisfied me beyond any reasonable doubt. The painting is his. Has been in his possession for years. And now, if you don't mind? I think Mrs Harris is wanting you back on the front row.'

He was obviously itching to have his own items assessed. Well, Lisa hadn't been too impressed with him in the first place. She looked round, perhaps a mistake as D C Wethers rapidly made his escape.

Lisa, however, had no intention of returning to her original seat. Oh, no, not when there was a spare place right next to the thief. The police might have shirked their duties and let him off the hook but there was no way she was going to.

She hurried back, knocking into people's bags and bundles and having to stop and apologise, which took even longer, but, yes, the seat was still there. And her quarry, gazing cheerfully around him as if he hadn't a care in the world.

Lisa sat down.

At least he looked startled, before the dark brows set in a frown.

'Oh, hello. So that's what that was about. Mrs Harris assured me you wouldn't be coming.'

Lisa glared at him.

'I'll bet she did. And when was this? When did you speak to Mrs Harris?'

Did this mean he knew who Lisa was? Had Mrs Harris told him?

'Three weeks ago, when I first agreed to come.'

Lisa frowned. He hadn't had the painting three weeks ago. That didn't make sense. But let that pass for a moment. Obviously some kind of delaying tactic.

'That is my painting,' she said grimly, waiting for him to produce some rubbishy excuse about finding it later and intending to return it to her publicly. 'I'd like an explanation, please, and my painting back.'

He shook his head, saying, 'This isn't your painting.'

'Nonsense. I've grown up with that painting. Of course it's mine. No-one else has ever been allowed to make a copy. There have been no prints published, not even any photos of it. It is a private and personal work, painted for and given to my mother.' Her voice was rising.

He folded his arms.

'I can prove it to you.'

'Yes? Well, be my guest.'

'There are two very important differences. One is in the title and the other is in the butterfly by the signature.' His voice was expressionless.

Lisa was staring at him, feeling the

colour draining from her face. He sounded so certain. And why would he be making this up? She didn't understand.

'Come and look.' He took her arm.

As if hypnotised, she was allowing him to pull her to her feet and guide her forwards, three steps, four, to where the painting was propped up on more blue cloths, centre stage and in pride of place. His voice seemed to be coming from a long way off.

'The title, you see. Yours is called *Gemini with Daisies and Forget-me-Nots*. This one is *Gemini with Forget-me-Nots and Daisies*. And if you look at the butterfly signature . . .'

She could see already. Why had she not noticed before? This butterfly was blue with glowing white wing tips. The one on their painting was white with blue tips. Small, subtle differences adding up to a major significance. She clutched at the edge of the stage for support.

'I don't understand.'

'Come and sit down.' His voice sounded sympathetic.

'I'm OK, thanks.' She wasn't quite ready to forgive him.

He sighed. 'This is the very last place I would have wanted you to go through this. But I thought you and your mother couldn't come. I asked Mrs Harris about that, in a roundabout way, and she assured me you wouldn't be here. And this is a charity my mother was always interested in. I knew Mrs Harris was looking for something big. I couldn't let her down.'

Lisa twisted away from him and went to sit down, keeping her back straight with an effort. If she didn't she might crumple into a hysterical heap, in front of everyone. It couldn't be possible, but it was. So she had to accept it. Her mouth was too dry to speak. She licked her lips and tried again.

'So where did this one come from?'

He paused, his voice wary.

'It was a gift, from your father. Look, it's a long story. We'd be better talking about it somewhere else, after this is over.'

There was something very, very wrong here. Part of Lisa didn't want to find out what it was. She had a dreadful feeling that the whole thing would be best left uncovered.

'I don't think so, thank you.'

'Think about it.'

She made a dismissive gesture with her hands, which could have meant anything, because now Mrs Harris was taking her position on stage. Even if they had wanted to talk further, the opportunity had gone.

For Lisa, the rest of the evening passed in a daze. She did register, however, that Robert, the art expert, was ecstatic about the painting, giving it a value that would have purchased a small house, far more than Lisa would have expected. They hadn't had theirs insured for anything like that much, even if the insurers agreed to pay up. And she hadn't contacted them yet. She was still hoping to avoid all that, wasn't she? After tonight's shock she didn't know what she wanted or what was feasible.

Mrs Harris introduced the young man as Mark Ridgely, and he explained that the painting had been a gift from the artist to his parents. The expert, Mrs Harris and the whole of the audience except Lisa accepted this without question.

Only Lisa knew that her father had not been in the habit of making gifts. Lisa and her mother had teased him about his habitual meanness.

Already Robert was holding Lisa's box and as Mrs Harris called her name, Lisa stood up without thinking and mounted the steps. It was fortunate that she'd practised her little speech because the words seemed to be coming out without conscious thought on her part.

They were carrying on with the Carlton Clive theme of course, were very lucky indeed to have his daughter with them tonight and the expert waved his sleeves, shaking his head at the impossibility of placing a value on such items and naturally she would never part with them, to which Lisa agreed.

'To any collector of Carlton Clive's works,' the expert was droning on, 'these would be a fascinating addition . . . '

But it was obvious, wasn't it, that the previously unknown painting was the real find? What would the expert have thought? What would anyone think, if it became generally known there were two of these paintings? Would the value of each be doubled? Not much point in thinking about that, since Lisa's was missing.

There was a great deal to think about and she didn't have long. Her first instinct was to reject Mark Ridgely's friendly offer. As she calmed down, however, she realised a further explanation was the only way forward. But she would set the time and place, thank you very much.

Not only about the painting and where it had come from. She wanted to know why Mark had been hanging around outside their house in the middle of the night. She wasn't going to let him off lightly.

The evening was now over. The audience was applauding. Lisa turned her head briskly.

'I have been considering your offer. Tomorrow for preference. How about lunch? Do you know the Crag View restaurant?' She added stiffly, 'It seems I've misjudged you, as well as putting you in a difficult position with the police. So we'll make this my treat. No arguments.'

He shrugged, nodding his acceptance.

5

Lisa didn't sleep well that night. Dozens of possibilities were buzzing around in her head. At one point she shot up in bed almost convinced that somehow Mark Ridgely could have altered the painting.

But, no, of course he couldn't. There was no mistaking the way her father had painted his titles, always blending the letters into the foreground. In her *Gemini*, the green brushstrokes almost merged with the blades of grass. You couldn't possibly alter it convincingly, not unless you possessed great skill.

When the morning came, she was no nearer coming to any decision. Why? Why had her father painted another *Gemini* and given it away, and to the Ridgely family? She had never heard of them before.

Something did emerge from the

hours of tossing and turning. A germ of an idea was beginning to form in her mind, something that might let her off her own personal hook, temporarily at least.

Lisa drove into the office well before nine. That way she could allow for the lunch break taking longer than usual. Also she booked a table. The Crag View was one of her favourites and only a few doors away from Philip's gallery. The thought of Philip being so near at hand for this difficult interview was reassuring.

She also phoned Mark's mobile number and asked if he would mind meeting her at the table. Not at all, he told her, taking the formal tone from her. That would be fine.

So that was organised. She drew a breath of relief, although she had less success in concentrating on the morning's work. She had been punctilious about her time-keeping, determined not to sell her employers short but was only too aware that she might as well have taken the morning off for all the good she was doing.

Almost a relief to leave and, hugging her coat around herself against a sudden spring chill in the damp air, she hurried through the steep, cobbled streets to keep her appointment.

Should she pop into the gallery first and tell Philip what she was doing? But it was already too late because here was Mark, approaching from the opposite direction. Surely that heart-stopping smile couldn't be for her?

Lisa's chest suddenly felt tight. Hardly surprising, she told herself, considering the reason for their meeting. Nothing at all to do with the smile. Somehow she had forgotten, since that night of the theft, how his smile had affected her.

As he held the door open for her, her legs were starting to feel weak.

'At least let me go halves,' Mark said, as they sat down. 'This is partly my fault. When I first suggested it, I wanted the lunch to be an apology.'

'Not a topic for discussion.' Lisa smiled back, not wanting to sound too brisk and bossy. She wouldn't get anything out of him that way. Because the more she thought about it, the more she was convinced her idea was the very best solution, if only Mark would go along with it. She added, 'We have so much to discuss already.'

'Yes.' He was glancing round at the beamed ceiling and terracotta-painted walls. 'I've never been here before. Very pleasant.'

'I've always found it satisfactory.' Oh, dear. How stiff and formal that sounded. 'Shall we eat from the set menu? It really is very good.'

'Fine by me.'

Lisa looked at him sharply. The way he was agreeing with everything was making her feel uneasy. She didn't know why. But she didn't want to waste time discussing the food. She dealt with the ordering as quickly as possible and Mark was still following her lead, making no objection when she refused the wine list, which was good, because she needed to give the whole of her attention to all this.

She placed her arms on the table, hands resting on top of each other and leaned forward.

'So, Mark, why did my father give your parents that painting? He was not a generous man. And the twin picture, as you now know, belonged, I mean belongs, to my mother.' She spread her hands wide, emphasising the question. 'Why?'

Mark's eyes were dark and serious.

'You've no idea how much I've thought about whether to tell you this. And when, and how. That was why I was hanging about round your house that night. I wanted to find out more about you. I thought it might help me to decide what to do. And as a friend had asked me to look after his dog while he was away, it seemed the ideal opportunity.'

Lisa was still ready to be suspicious.

'I didn't see a dog.'

'No, I know, but he was OK. He went home on his own.' Surprisingly, he grinned. 'I think he was fed up of doing the circuit past your house, up the hill, through the carpark, along the cobbles . . . When your alarm went off, that was the final straw.'

Mark looked round, as if hoping the waiter might arrive with something to distract them.

'I wasn't quite telling the whole truth, at the charity evening, neither to you nor to Robert. The thing is, Carlton Clive didn't give the painting to my parents. He gave it to my mother.'

'Oh,' Lisa said. This was it, the part she knew she didn't want to hear.

'She kept it wrapped up and hidden away at the back of the spare room wardrobe. That's why the colours are so bright. My father never knew she had it, even after their divorce, seven years ago.'

He paused, fiddling with his fork. Lisa couldn't see his face.

'I never knew. She only told me just

before she died and that was two years ago. She had cancer, you see. She said she had to tell me because I would find the painting and the resulting speculation would be worse for everyone.' He sighed. 'I've spent all this time wishing she hadn't told me and wondering what to do about it.'

'I still don't understand,' Lisa said. 'Why all the secrecy?' But she had a horrible churning feeling that she understood only too well. She stared blankly into the bowl of tomato soup that had appeared in front of her without her even noticing.

Both Mark's hands were on the table, fists clenched.

'I'm so sorry. I'd hoped to avoid all this. I really had.'

For Lisa, recognising the sincerity in his voice was no help. It didn't make things any better.

'Say it then,' she snapped, feeling close to tears. She wasn't sure whether the tears were for her mother or for herself, or for both of them.

He said softly, 'My mother and your father were having an affair. It lasted for years.'

Lisa put her hand over her mouth.

'So how did no-one find out about it?' She knew she sounded angry but couldn't help it. Somehow she had to control her fury but that wasn't easy. She was angry with Mark for telling her, with her mother for not knowing about this and most of all with her father for the colossal deception he had practised on all of them. Her only hope was that somehow Mark might have got it wrong. But she was certain that he had not.

Mark shrugged. 'I don't know. My mother used to visit elderly relatives a lot. I suppose that must have provided her with an excuse. As for your father, I can't say.'

She wanted to rage at him, sitting there with the strong features showing only regret. Why didn't he feel furious, too?

'You're taking this very calmly.'

'I've had two years to get used to it, don't forget. Believe me, I know how you're feeling. I found it incredibly difficult at first. If I could have got hold of your father, I'd have punched him.'

Lisa rested her elbows on the table, supporting her head with one hand.

'Why are you telling me now? I mean, I know I asked you, but couldn't the painting have stayed in your wardrobe, for ever if necessary?'

Why had her father done this, she wondered. Any of it? Why, if he had taken the trouble to maintain secrecy and so efficiently, why had he left this legacy of deception and betrayal?

All her memories of her father were darkened and spoiled.

It was as if someone had taken her mental picture and washed it over with a muddy grey blur. All the time he had been coming home to his loving, happy family, he had been leading this horrible secret life.

She had almost forgotten that she had asked a question. She lifted her head. Mark was sitting there, waiting for her. As if he did indeed understand exactly what she was going through, as of course he did.

He had been through all of this himself except that when he had found out, his mother had been dying which would have made it far, far worse. At least the wounds of Lisa's father's death were ten years old. She had been just fifteen.

He said quietly, 'I would have kept it hidden if I could, believe me. But now I need to sell.'

She couldn't stop herself.

'Oh, so greed is behind all this? I might have known.'

She knew as she spoke that she was being unfair but she had to hit out at someone and there was no-one else.

'No. Your father gave my mother the painting in case she was ever in financial need. He didn't think my father could be relied on to support her, and he didn't, of course. They got divorced, as I told you. This picture was for my mother to dispose of however she wished, if she had to.' He paused. 'Fortunately she didn't have to. She knew what that would entail.'

'You mean for myself and my mother.' Lisa's voice was stiff. 'But so do you. You know how difficult this will be for us, too.'

'Listen, if there had been any other way, believe me . . . ' He was frowning again. 'There isn't. That's why I gave in to Pamela Harris's persuasion and took it along. I needed a valuation. It seemed a good opportunity.'

'All very reasonable, I'm sure. You're making it sound as if you have no alternative. But that can't be true, surely.' Lisa knew she sounded petulant. She hadn't intended to say any of that. Shock, probably.

He shrugged. 'This isn't something I wish to discuss right now. You'll just have to take my word for it. I did try to get things moving in the most painless way possible. I made sure you wouldn't be attending the charity event. I was hoping for a discreet valuation and perhaps a quiet word afterwards with the expert about the best way forward.'

'Didn't you realise when Pamela Harris was talking you through the arrangements that discretion wasn't an option? Surely she told you about fast tracking the better items. Didn't that give you a clue?'

'I'm afraid I wasn't paying attention. And I'd no idea her expert would get so excited. I didn't know what the paintings were worth.' The deep brown eyes were staring intently into hers, obviously willing her to go along with him. 'So it was only fair to tell you my side of things. I couldn't see any way to avoid hurting you. But I hope you'll understand.'

'Yes, I do understand. But I don't want my mother to know.' And how could they manage that? But that was Mark's problem. Bad enough that their own painting had gone and that with every day that passed, the likelihood of their ever getting it back was lessening.

This was far, far worse.

Suddenly Lisa felt she couldn't take any more. She stood up.

'Excuse me a moment.'

She was reaching blindly for her bag, gesturing towards the Ladies.

Mark stood up, too, catching hold of her wrist.

'You won't run out on me, will you, Lisa? You will come back?' His voice sounded grim.

She pulled her hand away.

'Don't worry. I'm sure you'll get your money.'

She walked away between the tables, keeping her back and shoulders as straight as possible, hardly able to see where she was going.

Once making the Ladies, she leaned against the washbasins, surprised that her face looked so normal. Everything had changed in the last half hour, everything she had trusted and believed in. Mark had been right. She had no intention of going back. If she had ever needed Philip, she needed him now.

Thank goodness she had thought of choosing the Crag View, with the handy back way into the carpark.

She ran down the street, hardly able to contain the tears, and the elegant glazed door of the gallery was locked. She pushed hard with both hands, staring at it in disbelief. But of course, Philip could be out and about for all kinds of reasons, meeting clients, attending auctions and sales.

She should have phoned first and checked. She took a deep, sobbing breath. In her reflection in the glass, grief and shock were all too visible in her face.

She ran her hands through her curls. No shoulder to cry on. She was on her own. Come on, she told her reflection. Pull yourself together. You're being unfair. None of this is Mark's fault. In fact, he's doing his level best to cause as little distress as possible.

Inside the gallery, her eyes were suddenly drawn to one small painting standing on a display easel, a moorland landscape with two small figures, one of Carlton Clive's early works, before he began to concentrate upon the atmospheric portraits.

Yes, there was only one person truly deserving of her anger and she knew who that was, didn't she? Her father, whom she had idolised and remembered with love and fondness, but who had tricked his way into manipulating everyone's lives.

Gemini. Why had she never realised the significance of that strange title? Inappropriate for a painting of a girl on her own. She remembered asking her father about that. She had always thought it was a portrait of her mother, when she had been younger, slimmer. Certainly the hat was right.

Carol Clive still wore a hat like that for gardening in. But hats like that were common enough. And of course, you couldn't see the girl's face. Yet somehow, you gained the impression, in the way there was a lifting in the silhouette of her cheek, that the girl was smiling.

What was it she had asked her father?

'Why did you call it *Gemini* when Mum's birthday's in October?'

She had never understood her father's answer. He had smiled, not looking at her.

'There are two sides to everything. That's what the picture is about.'

Lisa had persisted. 'But what does it mean?'

The explanation had sounded very dull.

'When you're grown up, you'll realise that nothing is ever straightforward.'

Lisa had pouted, wanting a story; her father had his own wizardry in weaving stories around his paintings. But never for that one.

No, that painting had held a story too secret ever to be revealed, not until two of the people concerned were dead.

But her mother was still alive. Lisa knew she must protect her mother from this awful knowledge. She took a deep, strengthening breath. Besides, there was her plan to consider. She would not achieve anything by hiding away in here and feeling sorry for herself.

6

Lisa went back to the table filled with a new determination. Mark was sitting where she had left him, shoulders slumped and knife and fork arranged together on his plate. He looked lonely and vulnerable and had obviously given up on the meal. As a lunch, this had been a disaster. It was up to her to retrieve the situation, essential if her plan was to come to anything.

She rounded the table and Mark looked up and saw her. She was surprised at how the lines around his eyes lifted as he smiled his relief.

'I thought you weren't coming back.'

'I told you I would.'

'I know. I should have believed you but I could see how upset you were. Totally understandable, but there was no good way of telling you about all this. I didn't know what you'd be intending to do next.'

'Neither did I.' Lisa didn't sit down. 'Do you mind if we leave? I need to sort things out.'

He leaped up. 'Of course.'

'I need to walk. It helps me to think. I'll just see to the bill.'

She frowned, daring him to object.

He was silent as they went out into the street before turning, his hands outstretched.

'Can I meet up with you again? I don't like leaving you like this. I feel there's too much unfinished business.'

'Oh, no. I mean, yes.' Lisa was almost surprised into giving a nervous laugh. 'I meant we should both walk and talk and think, because I feel I owe you an apology, or several apologies. They seem to be escalating by the minute.'

She paused, pulling her collar up against the raw cold of the afternoon.

'Of course. That's why I wanted to meet up in the first place.' He hesitated, looking at his watch. 'But I'm afraid I don't have too much time.'

The damp was turning into a persistent grey drizzle and the streets were emptying. Lisa hardly noticed. Across the road from the restaurant, the hillside fell away steeply to the valley below. She frowned, as the scene seemed to tug at her memory. And, yes, of course, she knew now.

'We have to be farther along,' she said, half to herself, setting off swiftly, away from the buildings to find the half-remembered path, through the gap in the dry stone wall.

'Hang on,' Mark said. 'Where are we going?'

How could she explain the sudden compulsion to him?

'It isn't far,' she muttered.

He was following her without speaking. She wasn't sure if this was right, if she should share this with him. But the stone slabs of the old track were leading her through the wiry tufts of grass. A heap of stones loomed out of the mist and, yes, they were there. She paused, not knowing if he would understand, pushing her hands into her pockets.

'It's one of your father's paintings, isn't it?' Mark said slowly. 'The one on show in the Moorland Gallery. The one with the figures.'

'Yes,' Lisa whispered. 'Father and daughter.'

They stood staring out over the mist and hidden shapes.

'It wasn't like this when he brought me here,' she said softly. 'It was summer. But I shall always remember it.' She turned to look up at him, half expecting a cynical sneer but his gaze was full of understanding. 'He wasn't really a bad man, Mark.'

'I know.'

'I can't explain why he acted as he did.'

'Don't try.'

Lisa swallowed. Whatever was she thinking of? This wasn't doing anything to solve her main problem. She took a deep breath, trying to pull herself together.

'I'm sorry. I have an important

proposition to put to you. My mother will be coming home on Friday. By then, I'd been hoping to recover our painting and have it safely back in place. What I want to tell you is that I can see my way out of this. A way out of my problems anyway. I have a plan, if you'll agree to it.'

Without warning, the drizzle had become rain and was teeming straight down. Mark put his arm around her shoulders and hurried her towards the shelter of the rocks.

Lisa said, 'I should have brought an umbrella. And you haven't a coat. I didn't think. Walking was a bad idea.'

The words were tumbling over her tongue.

In the confined space of the dark boulders, Mark's face was unavoidably close to hers. And surely, she thought, gasping for breath, the space wasn't that confined? She could step back if she wanted to, away from what must be about to happen next. But she didn't want to step back. She moved her face towards his, only a fraction of an inch but knowing it was a signal. His breath was warm on her wet cheeks.

Their lips came together and Lisa forgot everything — where she was, how cold her feet were, the worry about the painting and her father's treachery, all swept away.

'I'm sorry,' Mark said. 'I shouldn't have done that.'

Lisa stared up into his face, still trying to put her feelings into compartments somehow. Would he kiss her again?

'We shouldn't have done that.'

All this emotion, she thought. It's affecting my judgement. Impossible to distance myself. I'm giving and receiving the wrong messages.

'You're confusing me, Lisa. I want to feel angry with you and I can't.'

'Angry?' Lisa stared at him. She had thought the anger should all be on her side. 'You've been concealing it very well.'

'I wanted to keep everything calm

and businesslike, but I'm attracted to you. And that isn't what I want. I can't let it happen. But whenever I look at you, I have to keep reminding myself that your father inflicted an illicit, hole-in-the-corner relationship on my mother for years. She deserved better than that. I thought I'd got over the bitter feelings but I haven't. Not altogether. They still keep surfacing when I least expect them.'

Lisa wanted to feel angry but she had to recognise the truth in what he was saying. None of this could have been easy for Mark either.

'I know.' Lisa's voice was shaky. 'That's exactly how I feel, although I'm viewing things from a different direction. I know what you mean. I almost wish I didn't.' Yet another dimension was revealing itself to her. She said, hesitantly, 'But if your mother was happy, Mark, doesn't that justify things? From your point of view anyway.'

He groaned. 'That's just it. She was happy. Everything tells me that she shouldn't have been but she was. She assured me of that.' He paused. 'As far as she could be, when someone else would inevitably be hurt by her actions.'

'Someone else? Oh, you mean my mother?'

'Yes. My mother was a kind and caring person. You have to believe that. She went through life doing her level best not to inflict pain on anyone, apart from this. That was something else I found so hard to understand. Somehow, her feelings for Carlton Clive had made her act completely out of character and I find it very difficult to forgive him for that, although apparently she believed what he told her about his relationship, that he was stuck in a cold and unhappy marriage and his wife didn't love him.'

Lisa gasped in horror.

'That wasn't true! That was never true.'

'I know. And before she died, my mother, Helen, had realised it wasn't

89

true and that Carlton Clive had deceived her. I'm sorry, Lisa, but your father caused all this pain just to get what he wanted.'

Suddenly Lisa didn't want to hear any more of this. She wiped tears from her face with the back of her hand.

'Stop it. How dare you criticise my father like that? Pretending to be so reasonable, but there were two people involved. It can't all have been his fault.'

'Lisa . . . ' He was trying to enfold her in his arms again.

'No!' She pushed him away. 'I've had enough.' She ran out into the driving rain, slipping and stumbling on the grit, heather scratching her ankles, hardly caring where she was going as she found the stone flags of the packhorse trail.

Distantly she could hear Mark's voice but she didn't stop, not until a rock rolled as she trod on it and her feet slid on the wet stone. She hit the ground, conscious of a bruising pain in her calf.

She lay there with the breath knocked out of her, staring at the grass, before closing her eyes and clenching a fist into her forehead. The fall had shocked the tears away. She wanted to lie here for ever, never facing up to the truth.

'Lisa! Are you OK?' Mark's arms were round her. She lacked the strength to push him back.

She muttered, 'Go away.'

He ignored her, helping her to sit up.

She gasped with pain as she tried to put the weight on to her right foot, collapsing against the wall.

'I'm fine,' she snapped.

'I don't think so.' Mark was feeling her calf and ankle with hands that were both strong and gentle. Lisa shivered. What was the matter with her? Why was she allowing this man to get close to her after what he had said about her father? But she already knew the answer and that everything Mark had said was true.

'Nothing seems to be broken. You may be able to stand if I help you.' His voice seemed abrupt. Lisa wondered guiltily if he'd known what she was thinking.

She tried to get up again, biting against the flash of pain as she put her foot to the ground.

'It's fine. I can walk. See?' She hobbled a few steps, determined to prove that she could, and overbalanced.

Mark's arms were there again, catching her as she fell.

'Don't be silly. We must have come half a mile at least.'

Before she could object he was stooping to slip one arm round her shoulders and another behind her knees.

'I'll carry you.'

'What? No, you can't.'

'Watch me.' Already he was jerking her off her feet and into his arms.

'Hey, no.' But already she knew her protest was futile. His suggestion made sense. She put her arm around his neck, merely to distribute her weight more evenly, she told herself. His face was close to hers, although he was staring ahead, as if concentrating on keeping his footing. It would be so easy, she thought, to brush her lips against his cheek until once again, her mouth found his. Stop it, she told herself sternly.

The intense anger of only moments before had disappeared. She no longer wanted to recapture it.

Now, she thought. It would be so easy to say, 'I'd like to borrow your painting.' She looked up, unable to read his face.

He was frowning against the rain, the dark hair wet against his forehead.

'Car keys,' he said abruptly.

'What?' She looked round, unable to believe they had moved so swiftly along the path but yes, here was the carpark.

'I need your keys so I can drive you. There's no way you can drive. Surely you have to admit that.'

'I won't know until I try.' It didn't seem likely as her foot was still throbbing. 'But what about your car?'

'I can get a taxi back to collect it.'

She didn't want to agree but this did seem the best solution. She sighed.

'All right.' She had to concentrate on concealing how much the manoeuvre of getting her into the passenger seat hurt. Otherwise he would be taking her to the nearest X-ray department and she didn't want that. It wasn't necessary. But, no, he was taking the route that would deliver her to her own front door. She waited for the advice that didn't come.

★   ★   ★

'If it's still hurting tomorrow, I'll get a taxi to the surgery,' Lisa said, fiddling for her house keys and knowing that her voice was defensive. Now he would be fussing around, wanting to come inside and make sure she was all right and she didn't want that either. Did she?

Mark grinned. 'I'm sure you will.' He was watching her open the door, making no move to come in.

'I'm fine now.'

'Absolutely.'

'You don't need to come in.'

'I won't, in that case.' He was already halfway to the gate.

'Hey,' she called after him. 'Didn't you want to ring for a taxi?'

'Mobile phone.'

Suddenly she remembered her request.

'I need to talk to you. I have to ask you something.'

He was striding down the slope of the drive as he turned his head.

'I'll be in touch.'

She glared after him. How had she let all the moves slip away like that? But there was nothing else she could do about it now. She would just have to wait.

7

By the following afternoon, she felt she could wait no longer. You would have thought Mark would be concerned about her foot, wouldn't you? When she'd told him, 'No fuss,' she hadn't meant to be taken so literally.

She knew exactly what she was going to say, too, that she felt much better and had known all along there was no need for concern. But if he didn't phone, her brave stance would be wasted.

The phone rang simultaneously with the doorbell and she chose the phone, reaching for it too quickly and collapsing into the nearest chair. Her foot wasn't as reliable as she'd thought. Anyway, she didn't want Mark to think she'd been waiting for his call.

'Come in,' she shouted.

'Hello, Lisa.' Philip was smiling as he

entered the room.

'Philip! Oh, it's you. Just let me deal with this.'

She had a momentary flash of disappointment. Ridiculous, she was always pleased to see Philip. But this meant she couldn't speak to Mark alone. Anyway, why should that matter, she asked herself.

She didn't want to draw attention to her ankle by hobbling off into the hall in search of privacy. She hunched over the phone, turning away.

'Yes?' If she had been expecting solicitous enquiries, she was about to be disappointed.

'I feel bad about yesterday's lunch,' Mark was announcing cheerfully. 'It wasn't much fun for either of us. To make amends and as I know you won't be on your feet as yet, I suggest that I come over and cook my speciality for both of us this evening.'

'What's that?' Lisa asked. Of all the stupid questions, she told herself. Here he was, making assumptions about what she wanted to do.

'Spag bol. It's the best.'

'That sounds great,' her mouth was telling him. 'But . . .'

'You're not doing anything else, are you?'

'Well, no.' She found herself grinning.

'See you soon, then. About half-five.' He rang off.

Lisa stared at the phone. Why was she smiling? He had hardly given her any chance to refuse. Talk about high-handed . . .

'Everything all right?' Philip asked.

'Oh, er, yes.' Lisa jumped guiltily. For a few moments, she had forgotten all about him. 'Just a business associate. Coming round later.'

'Ah.' Philip was looking disappointed. 'I had hoped, but never mind. I only came round on the off chance, mainly because I gather you were looking for me yesterday.'

'Was I? Oh, yes, of course.' Aeons ago, when she had wanted to speak to

him during the ill-fated lunch date
— she had almost forgotten. 'How did
you know?'

'I make a point of checking my
security camera footage. You can't be
too careful these days.'

'No, I suppose not.'

'And after your experience.' He
turned to look at the empty space on
the wall and sighed. 'If only Carol had
taken my advice and sold earlier. Still,
when you get the painting back, I'm
sure she will listen this time around.'

'Don't you mean *if* we get it back?'
Lisa muttered. 'Nobody seems to be
trying too hard.'

Philip smiled. 'These things take
time. Trust me. I do have my ear to the
ground, you know.' He sat on the sofa
beside her with sunlight gleaming on
the immaculate fair hair. 'Anyhow, what
was it you were wanting? Yesterday?'

'Ah. Well.' Yesterday she had been on
the verge of pouring her heart out to
him about everything. Today that
seemed impossible. Too much had been

revealed. She wasn't sure if she was ready to share her knowledge about her father with Philip.

And yet wasn't he the very person she should talk to? He had known her father and would understand. But it wouldn't be right to tell him when Carol didn't know. And it was Mark's secret, too.

'I was just passing,' she said lamely. 'I had lunch at the Crag View.'

Philip leaned forward, staring at her.

'Something's troubling you. I can tell.'

'No, not really,' Lisa said quickly. Too quickly.

He leaned forward to clasp her hands.

'If you only knew how much I want to share in your troubles. To protect you.' The clear blue eyes were staring straight into hers, as if he could read her thoughts. He said softly, 'I would very much welcome the opportunity to protect you for ever, Lisa.'

Her mind was spinning. She tried to

look away and couldn't.

'Protect me?'

His fingers were moving past her wrist to caress her arm.

'Yes. I would like you to consider me as more than a friend.'

Lisa wasn't ready for this. For some time, she had suspected that Philip wanted more than friendship. Until now she had cleverly evaded the issue but he had slipped under her guard. Her own fault for not telling him earlier where he stood. But how could she, when she hadn't known herself? And she still didn't know, not properly, how she felt about Philip or Mark?

She said, carefully, 'It's very kind of you to ask, Philip. I really appreciate this. But I don't know. It isn't something I can decide in a hurry.' She tried to smile. 'You've taken me by surprise.'

'Surely not? I'm merely voicing something that has been self evident for some time.'

'It's too soon,' Lisa said desperately. 'Although I do really appreciate everything you've done for my mother and myself.'

'What do I have to do, Lisa?' He paused. 'How about if I manage to get *Gemini* back for you?'

In spite of her feelings, she knew her eyes were lighting up.

'What? Could you? I know you feel the police should be left to get on with it, and you must have a lot of experience of how they cope with art theft, but really I'm not that confident. If you could help me, that would be brilliant.'

He was smiling at her enthusiasm but his eyes were still cold.

'One day, Lisa, you will have that look on your face for me. I promise you.'

Would she? Perhaps it wasn't so far fetched. She was grateful to him and he was everything anyone could ever want in a man, successful, good-looking, charming. Before she knew it, his arms were round her shoulders and his face was drawing closer. He was about to kiss her and, yes, she wanted that to happen. His lips had found hers. She closed her eyes.

Suddenly, the doorbell rang and Philip jerked away.

'Oh, no.'

Lisa tried to leap up, forgetting her ankle, and collapsed against the chair again. Giggling now, she turned to Philip. The laughter died in her throat at the look of fury in his eyes. No, surely she must have been mistaken.

He said, 'You're hurt.'

'It's nothing. Almost better.' No, she must have imagined his anger because he was back to being his usual pleasant self, the Philip she knew.

'I'll answer the door,' he was saying.

'No!' Lisa said. An unwelcome thought had occurred to her. She looked at her watch. Mark had said half past, hadn't he? But it was too late. As she struggled into the hall, Philip was already there.

'It's all right,' Lisa called. 'This is the business meeting I told you about, Philip. Philip, this is Mark. Philip was just going, Mark. He only popped in.' She gave Philip a hopeful smile. 'Perhaps you could come round again another time? I'll give you a ring. I'm really sorry.'

She tried to instil a huge range of meaning into the words.

'That's fine,' Philip was saying, looking Mark up and down. 'No problem.'

You couldn't have seen anything less like a business meeting, Lisa thought miserably, considering Mark was laden with supermarket carrier bags. And perhaps Philip would be less likely to want to help now. Oh, why had she felt so stupidly pleased to see Mark, when if Philip recovered the painting, she wouldn't need to tell Mark about her plan?

Too late to do anything about it. Philip was already down the steps, smoothing his cuffs, activating his car door locks. He turned, his expression unreadable.

'I certainly hope your meeting goes well.'

'Yes. Thanks.' She waved as the sleek black car swept down the drive, feeling that it was the least she could do.

Phew, Lisa thought, because she wouldn't want to alienate Philip and not only because of *Gemini*, but it was fine. Next time she saw him, she would explain. Perhaps by then she would have confided in her mother and everything would be out in the open.

Mark had already found the kitchen and was strewing ingredients across the surfaces.

'Have I arrived at a bad time? Sorry about that.' Lisa had the feeling he was trying not to laugh. 'I decided I might as well come straight over from the supermarket.'

'It doesn't matter.' Lisa knew that her voice sounded stiff. She felt her face growing hot as she remembered exactly what Mark had interrupted. 'It's good of you to offer to cook but there's really no need,' she said quickly, trying not to think about that moment when the doorbell had rung.

'There certainly is. This recipe is an old family secret, handed down through the generations. For my eyes only.'

Lisa stared at him for a moment before she laughed.

'And Ridgely is a well-known Italian name, is it?'

'Ah, well. Yes, you've got me there.' Mark didn't seem abashed. 'No, I'll come clean. You're supposed to be resting your ankle. You can sit and watch if you like. I enjoy talking while I'm cooking, but you haven't to move a muscle.'

Lisa sat down at the table.

'Agreed, although my ankle really is much better.'

'No arguing,' Mark said sternly.

He was moving quickly, doing everything with a dash of flair that was fascinating to watch. What would Philip be like in a kitchen, she wondered idly.

Neat and methodical, no doubt, if he ever cooked at all.

'That man who was just leaving?' Mark said suddenly. 'Does he come here often?'

'What?' Lisa jumped. 'What on earth has that to do with you?'

'Nothing, except I'm not too happy about you being alone here, not after everything that's happened. I was pleasantly surprised to see you had a friend round. Makes sense.'

'Yes, Philip's a very good friend,' Lisa said. 'More of my mother's than mine, really. He's an art dealer. Handles my father's paintings. We've known him for years.' She stopped. Why on earth was she saying this, as if she was putting herself out to make sure Mark didn't think there was anything between Philip and herself? But of course, there wasn't. Not yet.

'Good,' Mark said, stirring busily so she couldn't see his face. 'You need as many people dropping in as possible. But I'm still not sure that casual arrangements will be enough. I have a proposition to put to you.'

Where was this going? The conversation seemed to be sliding off out of control. Lisa said quickly, 'And I have a suggestion to put to you, too.'

Mark waved a spoon. 'Be my guest.'

Lisa took a deep breath.

'The thing is, I'd like to borrow your painting.'

'What?' Mark dropped the frying pan.

'Not for long,' Lisa said quickly. 'Only until my mother comes home and I've had a chance to break things to her gently. I'd like to protect her as long as I can. If there's a painting in the usual place when my mother comes in, I can choose the best time to tell her. The thing is, our sitting-room is fairly dark and if I remove the bulb nearest the painting, I'm sure she'll never notice.'

Mark said nothing.

'I understand if you're worried about security. But surely a house that has just been burgled will be completely safe.

The gang will know there's nothing else worth bothering with.'

'Of course I'm worried about security, yours mainly. Yes, I'll agree to it.'

'You will?' Lisa had been expecting to argue her case far more lengthily than this she could hardly believe it.

'On one condition,' he went on, 'that *Gemini* and I come as a package. That I stay here to look after it.'

'Oh.' Part of her was leaping about joyfully thinking what a wonderful idea. Be sensible, she told herself. This is a business arrangement, just as she'd told Philip. But she could hardly refuse if she was seriously expecting Mark to take such a risk.

'I think that would be quite a good idea,' she said cautiously.

Mark grinned. 'That's settled then. I can go back and get her straight after we've eaten.'

'Hey, no. Mum isn't due back for a day or so. That isn't necessary at all.'

Mark's eyes were dark. His face was serious.

'You've forgotten my proposition. I was going to suggest I moved in for a day or so to look after you.'

'What? Me? But that's . . . ' She'd been going to tell him how ridiculous that was. Hardly fair, however, when he would be doing her such a big favour. 'I don't need looking after,' she mumbled.

'No?' His gaze was directed towards her ankle. 'You're hardly in a fit state to look after yourself at present. I was thinking about it last night. I should never have left you on your own here.'

'I was fine.'

'Yes, as it happens. Anyway, shall we agree that I'm coming here to look after the painting and I'll bring it round tonight? And if I happen to watch over you, too, at the same time, that will be incidental.'

'All right.' Lisa sighed. It wasn't worth arguing about, and somewhere below her ribs, a warm feeling was growing at the thought of having Mark in the house. Strictly a business arrangement, she told herself quickly.

'What about the insurance?'

'Don't worry, I'll check my policy.'

Here I am, Lisa thought gloomily. Rushing in again, without thinking of the sacrifice Mark would be making if his painting was stolen, too. She was quiet for a while, as Mark finished preparing the meal and served it on to the plates.

'This is great, Mark. You're a brilliant cook.' Lisa only wished she didn't have so many other things to think about and could appreciate it more. She said suddenly, 'How would we explain your being here? My mother would wonder why we were suddenly becoming so security conscious. I don't want to draw her attention to your painting.'

Mark was grinning. 'We could say I'm your new boyfriend.'

'No way, that's asking too much of you. That isn't fair. Not on top of everything else.'

Mark paused with a forkful of spaghetti in the air midway between them. She wondered if he was going to aim it at her mouth instead of his.

'If you agreed to come out with me again, it might be halfway to being true.'

In spite of everything, she almost laughed at the effrontery of it. But the suggestion did make some kind of sense.

'I suppose so. Not the part about it being true,' she added hastily.

'Let's face it, there's still a lot that we have to talk through, like, your father was a huge part of my mother's life. I'd like to know more about him. And recovering your painting, I want to help you with that. Two heads are better than one. Have you tried the internet?'

Two men and two kisses, Lisa was thinking, both completely different. Mark's rainswept and passionate, Philip's skilful and considered. Stop that, she told herself, and brought her thoughts back to the moment.

'You're right. We do have a lot to discuss. Strictly business. Agreed?'

'Yep. Sorry.' She didn't think he

sounded too sorry. If he, too, was remembering their kiss, she could hardly blame him. With this half-and-half relationship she seemed to be slipping into, she no longer knew what she wanted and where this was going.

8

Mark paused at the front door, saying, 'I'll be straight back before you know it. Don't worry about making up a bed, not with that ankle. I'll bring my sleeping bag and camp out on the sitting-room floor. The best burglar deterrent around.'

Lisa nodded. She was allowing the door to take her weight, ready to lock it behind him. He didn't seem in any hurry to go.

'I took advantage of the emotional state you were in yesterday,' he said quietly. 'I shouldn't have done.' He leaned forward and she waited, holding her breath. His lips were within inches of brushing her forehead.

No, she couldn't allow this to happen. One thing at a time. Lisa drew back, smiling.

'If I'd thought that, I'd have stamped

on your foot. I've got a mind of my own, you know.'

'I should hope so. But it wasn't fair. Let's concentrate on the painting for now, shall we?'

★   ★   ★

'There.' Mark stood back as *Gemini* was finally placed in position. As if it had been there for years, Lisa thought, fitting perfectly into the rectangular shape of faded crimson on the wallpaper. Her father must have had the two framed at the same place. But the colours were clearer and brighter, the daisy petals possessed a white sheen, the forget-me-nots sparkled and the sunlight had a pristine, just-risen quality.

'Much better here than in the wardrobe,' Mark said.

'Yes.' Lisa felt satisfied and tearful, both at once. 'Thanks. You don't know how much this means.' What was she thinking of? She had been one step away from giving him a thankful hug. No way. She would have to watch herself. He would be getting the wrong idea. She said briskly, 'I've phoned into the office and told them about my ankle. They're not expecting me in tomorrow. So you won't have to worry about the painting being alone in an empty house.'

'I'd thought of that myself. I'm due a few days off. Now seemed a good time to take them.'

'Oh.' Lisa frowned. She hadn't realised just how seriously he would be taking his guard duties. 'There's no need. Really.'

'I think there is. You're forgetting the bit about needing protection yourself.' She opened her mouth to protest and he silenced her by placing a finger across her lips.

'No, I'm not willing to take the risk. You couldn't get away from a would-be thief at present.'

Lisa removed his hand.

'I'll be fine tomorrow. Particularly

after a good night's sleep.'

'We'll argue about that in the morning, shall we?'

Lisa nodded. Obviously this was a dismissal and she wasn't sure whether to be relieved or sorry. Once again, she didn't know what she wanted.

'I'll help you up the stairs.' Mark's tone of voice was not allowing for any argument.

'That's not necessary. I got up and down last night with no bother.' Not quite true as she had taken each step one at a time and had been panting with the effort before she reached the top. 'Hey!' she exclaimed because once again he was sweeping her up into his arms. 'You'll overbalance,' she said furiously. 'This isn't a good idea. Put me down.' But already they were more than halfway.

Soon he was setting her down gently on the landing. She felt a pang of disappointment, just below her ribs. His eyes were close to hers and alight with laughter. She had a horrible feeling he knew exactly what she had been thinking.

'You'll be OK from here.' It wasn't a question.

'Yes. Thank you.' She was trying to recapture her dignity and, she suspected, failing miserably.

'I'll see you in the morning then. Sleep well.' He turned and strode down the stairs.

In the morning, Lisa was up and dressed early to get down the stairs on her own. So it was disappointing to find Mark already in the kitchen.

'Coffee and toast?' he asked as she limped in, trying to demonstrate how well she could walk although the ankle seemed to have stiffened in the night. It would soon wear off. She would tell him so. But he didn't ask.

'Toast will be fine, thank you.'

She sat down at the kitchen table. How on earth were they going to spend the day, she wondered. But, of course, she could get on with her research. She could ask Mark to fetch the boxes she needed to tackle next.

As if reading her thoughts, Mark said, 'I've brought something of mine to get on with while I'm here, if you've got a socket in your garage.' He was searching for plates in the cupboard so Lisa couldn't see his face. But something in his voice told her this was no ordinary DIY project.

'Yes, fine. Are you repairing something?'

'Not as such.' He turned to face her, putting a pile of plates on the table. Too many but Lisa didn't say anything. 'I'm a sculptor. That's why I work at the factory. They let me have metal off-cuts for free.' He nodded as if coming to a decision. 'Wait here, I'll show you. I've got one in the boot.'

Before Lisa had time to reply he was out of the kitchen door. She didn't know what to expect. How big would it be? In moments he was back, holding the metal sculpture easily in his hands and set it down on the table.

Lisa stared at the dark, writhing

shapes, fascinated. At first she thought they were purely abstract, beautiful but without any particular meaning. Gradually, she realised the shapes were two leaping animals and the curving lines of their backs gave the sculpture a particular grace.

'They're dogs, aren't they?' she said at last. 'Mark, they're amazing. But I had no idea. Do you sell many?'

He grinned. She had never seen him looking self-conscious before. Obviously her praise had meant a great deal to him.

'Haven't tried yet. But I intend to.'

'Yes,' Lisa said thoughtfully. 'I must introduce you to Philip. He might be able to help you. He sells my father's paintings for us. I forgot, you've already met him. Perhaps that wouldn't be such a good idea after all.'

Mark didn't seem to notice anything.

'Yes, that would be great. Any contact will help. And speaking of contacts, there's something else I want to check out before I get started on my finishing touches to this. How long have we got?'

Lisa blinked at the change of subject and said, 'Sorry?'

'To find the painting. Before your mother comes home.'

'Not long. She's due back on Friday.' How could she forget, even for a moment? It was like a black cloud hanging over her.

'Don't worry. We'll give it our best shot. I'm going to try the internet for starters. And e-mailing some art dealers. It's worth trying.'

At last, Lisa thought, someone else who believed in direct action. As they both continued with their respective tasks, the day passed swiftly. She had to admit to herself that she liked having him around. For security purposes only, of course.

'Perhaps we're going about this the wrong way,' Mark said a while later, coming in from the garage and frowning towards the computer screen. 'I've just had an idea.'

Lisa was in the middle of arranging a

number of sketches in date order.

'Mmm?'

'Since my painting is here, why don't we use it? Instead of suggesting I'm in the market for buying your *Gemini*, why don't I put it around that it's been recovered and is here?'

Lisa stared at him.

'What for? My mother isn't going to check it out with the art dealers.'

'Because one person will know that we're lying. The thief. And he might well take action.'

'What?' Sketchbooks skittered off Lisa's knee. She hardly noticed. 'You mean, use your painting as bait?'

'Exactly.'

'But you can't. It's too risky.'

'I don't think so. You saw him, didn't you? There was only one man. I can get a couple of workmates down here for a night or two, to share the guard duty. Let's face it, we've got a very good chance of recovering the painting before Friday.'

He stood up and placed his hands on

her shoulders, his face alight with enthusiasm.

'It can't fail. No, I want to do this. A way of righting the past wrongs between our two families.'

The more Lisa thought about it, the more she was tempted. And when Mark's face was so near hers, she found resistance impossible.

'You can spend the night at my flat,' Mark was saying. 'That way I'll know you're safe.'

'Oh, no,' Lisa said firmly. 'I'll agree to be on hand upstairs, with my mobile phone, to ring the police. But I'm not moving out. Not for anything.'

He sighed. 'OK, then. There'll be no risk to you. Not with the rest of us down here. We'll set everything up for tomorrow night to begin with. There should be enough time.'

* * *

When Lisa met Gary and Brian from the factory, she had to share Mark's confidence. They were polite, cheerful and very broad shouldered.

By the third night, however, she had to admit they had tried and failed. She stayed awake as long as possible but each morning she woke to the disappointment of discovering that nothing had happened.

'We should never have started this,' she told Mark gloomily. 'How are we going to explain the presence of these two. You can't all be my new boyfriends.'

'We'll say there have been burglaries in the area and you were concerned,' Mark said cheerfully. 'That's true, at least.'

Fortunately Lisa didn't have to drive over to North Wales again to collect Carol. Jenny Palmerston had re-arranged the whole thing.

'Absolutely no need for that,' Carol Clive had said. 'Jenny is visiting relatives in York and can easily make a slight detour from the motorway to drop me off.'

Things got off to a good start when Mark came out to Jenny Palmerston's car to help with the bags and Jenny was swept in for a swift cup of tea. Bobby was dancing round everyone's feet and rushing off to explore his favourite haunts in the garden and the garage and there was so much bustle and turmoil there could surely be no time for anything else.

'Goodness,' Carol Clive said, 'and you've re-arranged the chairs. Yes, I think I approve. What a lot of changes. You'd think I'd been away for six months. New boyfriend, new layout, you have been busy.'

'Would you like a cup of tea, Jenny?' Lisa asked.

'How very kind,' Jenny was saying. 'And this must be the new boyfriend. Your mother was thrilled to hear about that on the phone. Come and sit down beside me, Mark, and tell us all about yourself. Carol is dying to know.'

Oh, dear, Lisa thought. This was a danger she hadn't anticipated. She would have to get the kettle on at the speed of light and be back to rescue her supposed boyfriend.

Behind Jenny's back, Mark was grinning and mouthing, 'Don't worry.'

'Sorry, Jenny,' Lisa's mother said. 'I've no intention of subjecting Mark to the Spanish Inquisition just yet.'

Jenny Palmerston was not to be put off that easily.

'So you only met him last week, Lisa? Carol was telling me about it. Seems as if he's becoming a permanent fixture already.'

'I'm sure Lisa knows what she's doing. She usually does.' Carol was smiling. 'Look, my legs have stiffened up with sitting in the car for hours. I'd rather be walking about. Why don't I make the tea?'

'If you're sure,' Lisa said, sitting down quickly and hiding a smile at the disappointment on Jenny's face. Probably trying to see the funny side of Jenny was the only way. Otherwise, she would drive you mad. Before Jenny could ask any more questions, Lisa launched into a description of what Mark did and how they had been out for lunch and attended Pamela Harris's charity event, topics that seemed safe.

'Oh, Pamela Harris, of course.' Carol's face lit up, catching the end of Lisa's sentence as she came in with the tea-tray. 'You were going to take those things of Carlton's, weren't you? Did they go down well?'

Jenny stood up. 'And of course, this is the painting you told me about. Superb, I must say. I'm surprised Pamela Harris didn't try to persuade you to take this to her event. She always was the pushy sort.'

Lisa could feel her heart speeding up.

'I'm sure she would have done if she'd thought about it. But what have you been doing all week, Mum? I'm dying to hear all about it. And a new hair-do. It looks really nice. Those highlights suit you.'

'Gemini with Forget-Me-Nots and

Daisies,' Jenny was murmuring.

As long as she stayed over there and kept to murmuring, Lisa thought. She edged her chair a few inches to the left and her mother was obliged to turn her head away from Jenny and *Gemini* to answer her daughter.

'Jenny's idea,' her mother said. 'I must admit, a new look was long overdue.'

Oh, no, now she was standing up to check her hair in the mirror over the sideboard. Try something else.

'So where did Jenny take you? I thought we'd covered the area pretty thoroughly but I'm sure Jenny knows all the places tourists usually miss.'

Lisa raised her voice a little but without looking at Jenny, hoping that the other woman would be unable to resist taking part in this conversation.

Unwittingly, Carol came to her aid.

'Your tea's here, Jenny. You don't want it to be getting cold.' Yes, Jenny was giving the painting a last glance and coming over to sit down.

Lisa breathed a sigh of relief. Crisis averted.

Fortunately, Lisa's mother seemed every bit as eager as Lisa to send Jenny on her way.

'Don't feel you have to hang around on my account, Jenny, when I know you have a long drive ahead of you, and when you were so determined not to accept my offer of an overnight stop.' Carol Clive hesitated politely. 'Although the offer still stands if you've changed your mind.'

Lisa tried to turn her sharp intake of breath into a cough and almost choked. Oh, no, she couldn't. Not on top of everything else. Jenny's eagle eyes would be peering into every corner, jumping to every possible conclusion. She didn't dare look at Mark.

But thankfully, Jenny was leaping to her feet.

'Goodness me, no, that would be time wasted. And it's barely an hour to my journey's end. Sorry to disappoint you but I must be adamant.'

'I'm so sorry, Mum,' Lisa said as they waved the car away. 'I had no idea. If I'd realised Jenny was only just around the corner, ready and waiting to bump into you, I would never have left.'

Carol laughed. 'Luckily for me, I knew only too well, as soon as I saw her. I could have avoided her, but I approached her. I wanted to know if I could cope with her any better now than when I was seventeen and she trampled all over me. In a well-meaning way.' She sighed. 'Poor Jenny, because she does mean well. And now . . . ' She turned to Lisa, smiling.

Lisa said quickly, 'Do you want to unpack? I'll take your cases upstairs.'

'No, no, let me,' Mark said.

'Talking of knowing what's best for oneself, no, thanks, I'll have another cup of tea. And you can come and sit down, both of you, and talk to me. Please?' She ushered Lisa and Mark politely but firmly into the front room and closed the door. 'Now, I would very much like to know, Lisa, why Helen Ridgely's son is suddenly your boy-friend and why Helen Ridgely's *Gemini* painting is on my wall?'

9

Mark and Lisa were both staring at her like guilty children. Lisa glanced longingly at the closed door. No escape.

'But I don't understand,' she faltered. 'I didn't know you knew anything about any of it.'

'I've known for years. I could only survive with your father by knowing everything he did.' Carol's voice was crisp but firm. 'And what he wouldn't tell me, I made sure I found out. Private detectives, mainly. There were a great many women to find out about, right from the start. Nothing, I eventually decided, to worry about much because none of them lasted long.'

She paused. 'Except for your mother, Mark. She was my greatest rival, my greatest worry. After a while it became obvious that even she, intentionally or not, wasn't going to upset things for Lisa and me, not even when her marriage broke up and she got her divorce. Oh, that was a dreadful time for me. The uncertainty, the not knowing, because Carlton would only talk to me about his affairs when they were over, coming to me filled with regret and apology. And he never told me about your mother, Mark.'

She closed her eyes, leaning back against the dark red sofa cushions.

'That was how I knew what a danger she presented to me and my marriage.'

Mark's voice was quiet.

'I'm not excusing her but I don't think it was entirely her fault.'

'Goodness, no. It wouldn't be. I know it takes two but when Carlton had made his mind up, resisting his charm was incredibly difficult. I know that myself. And for someone in a marriage that was already unhappy . . . But you see, he always came back to me, until I outlived them both.'

She paused, brushing a hand across her face.

'Oh, Mum.' Lisa put her arms round her.

'Don't be feeling sorry for me, dear. That's all in the past now.' Carol sat up, rearranging her sleeves. 'I didn't intend to say any of that. I wanted answers to my questions before I started on yours. What I do want to know is, where is my painting?'

There was no help for it. Lisa swallowed and came straight out with it.

'I'm so sorry. I'm afraid it's been stolen.' She bowed her head, hardly daring to look at her mother's face, knowing how upset she would be.

Once again Lisa's mother rose to the occasion.

'Stolen? I see. I suspected as much, as soon as I realised you'd made the switch. My own fault. Far too great a temptation to have something like that in an ordinary home. I should have sold when I had the chance.'

'But, Mum, I don't understand. You've always loved it so much.'

'Loved it?' Carol Clive gave a short laugh. 'When every time I looked at it, the painting reminded me of my rival? I'm sorry, Mark, but I'm sure you knew this wouldn't be easy.'

Mark nodded, his face solemn.

'Yes, I did know. Nobody pushed me into this.'

Carol was saying, 'And reminding me of how Carlton was so two-faced, in giving us the twin paintings. It was a game to him. And a cruel one at that. No, I've been foolish keeping it. Whenever I looked at it, I felt sad and angry. High time I grew up, moved on and put all that behind me.'

Lisa felt a wave of sadness. Her mother was talking about a stranger. Lisa felt as though she had never known her father at all, or not the man Carol was talking about. After little more than a week, she knew Mark far better than she had ever known Carlton Clive.

It was almost a relief when the doorbell rang, jarring through Lisa's unwelcome thoughts. Carol's expression slipped for a moment. In spite of her brave face, the revelations couldn't have been easy. She must have known for years that this moment would catch up with her one day.

'It's OK, Mum,' Lisa said quickly. 'Whoever it is, I'll send them away. I'll say the drive over gave you a headache.'

'Not so far wrong,' Carol murmured with a small smile, 'but it was the driver rather than the drive.'

Lisa laughed but knowing, as she caught Mark's eye, that she was not convincing him. Already he knew her well enough to guess at her real feelings.

She didn't want this. And it wasn't fair on Mark either but she couldn't ask him to leave yet, because of the painting. But wait a minute, now that her mother knew everything, there was no need for either Mark or the painting to stay.

She flung the front door open and the dismissal faded before she'd begun. She was looking at two large bouquets of flowers.

'Oh!' Automatically, Lisa opened her arms to receive them, unable to see the deliveryman's face, not realising until she had committed herself to taking them that the legs beneath the bouquets were wearing a smart, dark suit and there was a familiar large gold signet ring on one finger.

'For you and the lovely Carol,' Philip said. 'To welcome her home to what I know will have been a grave shock. And a bouquet for you, too, to ensure that you're bearing up.'

'That's very kind.' Unbalanced by the weight of the cream-coloured lilies, Lisa was stepping backwards and Philip was stepping forwards and somehow he was in. 'I'm sorry, Philip, but Mum's only just got back, minutes ago, and she's very tired. Has a severe headache, in fact.'

She knew that the words sounded churlish when he'd made this magnificent gesture. The flowers were tickling her nose. She looked around the hall wildly, wondering where to put them down. There was only the floor and that didn't seem right.

Philip, taking advantage of her dilemma, was past her already.

'Only for a moment,' he was saying with cheerful determination. 'To pay my respects in this time of trouble.'

'No,' Lisa cried. 'Don't go in there.'

Too late because he was already opening the sitting-room door, saying, 'I'll be very quick, I promise you.'

Lisa hurried after him, hampered by the armfuls of vegetation.

'Mother, Philip isn't stopping but he's brought us these beautiful flowers. Isn't that kind?'

Philip had stopped abruptly. Already he was looking past Carol and Mark, to the fireplace wall. In the back of his neck, a nerve was twitching.

'Philip!' Carol said, leaping up swiftly in a way that made the headache story seem less than convincing. 'How very thoughtful.'

'Yes, I told him you weren't feeling too well,' Lisa said. 'He's just popped in to see how you are.'

'You've got it back.'

Philip's voice sounded as if he was talking through a dust mask.

'Oh, yes.' Lisa glared at him. What was he playing at? He'd had no idea her mother knew it had ever been stolen. As it happened, the fact that Philip had blurted it out didn't matter too much, but he wasn't to know that.

Mark was rising to his feet, hand stretched out and creating a diversion.

'I don't think we've met properly. Mark Ridgely.'

'Ah. No.' Philip turned his head slowly away from the painting.

At last, Lisa thought. He seemed to be getting it now. Better late than never, she supposed. She laid the flowers down on the sofa. No way was she leaving the room in order to take them anywhere else, not even to shove them in a plastic bucket in the kitchen. Mark's diversion was proving a success. Well done him.

'And now I'm afraid I'll have to show you out, Philip. I'm sorry,' Lisa said firmly. 'But I'm sure you'll be able to come and visit properly tomorrow. And we'll be able to give you our full attention.'

By then they would have decided what they were going to tell him. Unfortunate that he had seen Mark's painting but she was sure they would come up with something, even the truth. But that needed careful consideration.

Carol was sinking back on to her chair, dabbing her forehead with a tissue.

'So kind, Philip, but, yes, if you wouldn't mind. I'm sure I'll be better tomorrow.'

Philip now seemed more than willing to be ushered back into the hall and for the sitting-room door to be closed behind him. But once there, he planted his shiny black shoes on the tiles and it was obvious he was not going any farther — not yet.

'So does this Mark Ridgely have some kind of medical qualification?'

'Sorry? Er, no. He's in engineering. He makes bolts.'

'I merely wondered why your mother had sufficient stamina to be having a conversation with a man who makes bolts, someone I, as a frequent visitor to your home, have never heard her mention before. I think I deserve an explanation.'

Lisa felt tempted to tell him it was none of his business to whom her mother chose to talk. But making him angry wouldn't help. At all costs she must avoid telling Philip about the painting until they had their story up and running. It wouldn't be fair to include anyone else in the truth without her mother's permission.

Lisa said, 'I'm seeing him.'

Philip stared at her.

'You mean, you're going out with him?'

'Yes.' Lisa suddenly felt like grinning with delight. She tried to control her mouth though she had a horrible feeling it was performing face-pulling contortions and all on its own.

'So the other day, when I wanted to take you out, purely to cheer you up because I knew how badly you would be feeling, that man wasn't here for a business discussion at all?'

'No, we were having a business discussion. He's a sculptor as well. He makes these wonderful sculptures out of metal off-cuts. We were having a discussion about how he might place his work.'

Philip was raising his eyebrows.

'Seems strange that you should have been in such a hurry to send me away in that case. My expertise might have been helpful.'

'Er, that's right. Yes. Well, I didn't know what the discussion was going to be about, not at that point.'

Lisa knew she was tangling herself in knots, as well as sounding overly apologetic and that was silly. She had nothing whatsoever to apologise for.

'Whoever I go out with is my decision, Philip.'

He snapped his head back.

'Of course it is. Let me get this straight. You wanted to introduce your mother to the new boyfriend as soon as possible. Perhaps I may deduce that the encounter has not been a welcome one because I think I can say she and I had reached an understanding as far as your happiness and future are concerned. No wonder she isn't feeling well after such a shock.'

Lisa took a deep breath. An understanding about her happiness and future? She sincerely hoped he didn't mean what that sounded like. The cheek of the man.

Surely he couldn't possibly have mentioned anything of the sort to Carol before receiving an acceptance from

Lisa herself. No, keep calm. She must have misunderstood him.

'I realise I may have hurt your feelings but I think we should stop this right now. Otherwise one of us will be saying something we may regret very much indeed, and I might feel obliged to withdraw my mother's invitation for tomorrow, on her behalf.'

Philip was putting a hand to his face.

'You're right. I'm not myself. Too much to take in.' By now Lisa was successfully edging him to the front door. 'But, the painting. I'd heard rumours but I dismissed them. Did the police find it? And why on earth didn't you let me know?'

'It's only just happened,' Lisa said quickly. 'I didn't have time. And I'm sure I'll be able to tell you everything tomorrow. You'll see.'

At last he was allowing her to usher him out. She closed the door behind him as soon as he had crossed the doormat, almost scraping the backs of his heels.

Leaning against the wooden panels, she listened to the noise of his car driving away, making quite sure he had really gone before re-entering the sitting-room.

'Poor Philip,' her mother said. 'You were very hard on him, Lisa. No help for it, of course. I knew why, and thank you.'

'Bad timing or what? If only he'd phoned first. We could have put our heads together and decided what we were going to tell him.'

'You're not going to tell him the truth then?' Mark asked.

'I don't know. But I couldn't just then. It wouldn't have been fair. I have to discuss it with both of you first.'

Mark shrugged.

'He'll have to know eventually.'

Her mother was smiling and shaking her head in bemused admiration.

'I really think Mark must be a good influence on you, Lisa. Is this the daughter who has spent her life rushing in and regretting it later? I can't believe how cautious you're being.'

'I only rush in on my own account,' Lisa said. 'Not when I could hurt somebody else. And I don't want to hurt either of you two.'

Mark was frowning.

'Let me get this straight. Philip is the same art expert you told me about?'

'That's right.' Lisa's thoughts were spinning once more. Once again she had sent Philip away for no good reason. But could she ever regard Philip as anything other than a friend?

'Why, Mark?' Carol asked, leaning forward as if she was aware that Mark's question had been for a purpose. 'Have you thought of something?'

'Only for myself. Philip could be very useful in selling my painting. He could give me an idea of what the demand might be, and even help in drumming up a demand.'

'Of course he will,' Carol said. 'He's exactly the person you need. So you are selling, are you?'

'I have to.' Mark looked regretful.

'My mother's last wish was that it should eventually be sold in aid of her favourite charity. I'm afraid they need the money.'

'Oh, Mark,' Lisa said. 'Was that why? Why didn't you say? I was horrible about that.'

Mark shrugged awkwardly.

'I should have done but the whole thing was getting to be too much.'

'Of course you must dispose of it.' Carol parted her hands and closed them again. 'Helen had exactly the right idea about that. I thought I would keep our last painting for you, Lisa.' Her voice softened. 'Because you idolised your father, and I didn't think it would be fair to tell you the truth about him.'

She stood up and began pacing up and down in front of the fireplace, glancing at the painting as she spoke.

'One day, I would, I told myself, when you were older or when you fell in love, because then you would be more likely to understand.' She smiled. 'And perhaps it's happening already.' She was looking at Mark.

'What?' Lisa was only realising in slow motion what her mother was getting at. 'Oh, no. Don't hassle Mark. You'll frighten him off.' She bit her lips. 'No, that wasn't what I meant to say.'

Fortunately Mark was grinning at her.

'I think Lisa means we haven't known each other very long. It seems a bit soon to be making a commitment.'

'Sometimes one glance is all it takes, one of those across-a-crowded-room moments. I'm a very good judge of character. Mark strikes me as one of those people you feel you've known for a very long time, even after only ten minutes.' Carol raised her eyebrows at Lisa. 'But whatever you say.'

'Don't be mapping out my life for me, Mum.' First Philip and now Mark.

'As if I would.' Carol's face was bland. 'But whatever happens between the two of you, I'm glad you introduced us. Meeting Mark is putting something right that should have been healed long ago, if I'd had any sense. And I would like to welcome Mark here any time.' She smiled at her daughter. 'As a friend, of course.'

Lisa raised her eyebrows at Mark.

'I'm very pleased to see that you've achieved the Motherly Seal of Approval.'

'Yes, I knew you would be,' Carol Clive said, ignoring the sarcasm. 'And now, can we decide what we're going to tell Philip?'

10

To Lisa's surprise, Carol threw herself into Mark's plan with enthusiasm.

'What, take your *Gemini* back home? And before we've achieved anything? Oh, no. I want to be in on this. Surely we can manage a night or two more.'

Lisa and Mark looked at each other and shrugged.

'If you like,' Lisa said carefully. As their plan hadn't worked there could be no possible danger. And Carol had responded so well to everything they had thrown at her that it seemed unkind to refuse.

'Will Gary and Brian be willing to drop round again?'

Mark said, 'As long as it takes, they told me.'

'Let's make tomorrow our last night,' Lisa suggested. 'After that, Mark can take his painting off to the nearest bank vault before he puts it up for sale.' She would be relieved when that happened, although the house would seem empty without Mark's presence.

Carol was frowning and drumming her fingers on the arm of her chair.

'I feel bad about excluding Philip. I know you were protecting me but he deserves a full explanation and the sooner the better. It's only fair. I'll get hold of him on his mobile and ask him to come straight back.'

Lisa sighed. 'No, I'll do it.' She, too, was feeling guilty at how she had deceived Philip by not telling him everything but for now, Philip would be more useful to them if he didn't know about the plan. Philip was so honest he would be hopeless at putting out inaccurate information, even if he believed in the cause.

'And I'll see him on my own. It's my fault so it's up to me to put things right.'

Discouraging her mother's presence at the interview with Philip was far easier than persuading Mark that he wasn't required. Her mother had finally gone upstairs to unpack and Mark was voicing his concerns.

'I have to try and convince Philip that we've recovered our painting,' Lisa said quietly. 'The slightest hint of you being here and he'll put two and two together. Everything has to seem normal.'

'I don't like it,' Mark muttered. 'I'll be in the kitchen, near at hand. Just in case.'

'In case of what? I'm a modern woman. I can take care of myself. And it's only Philip. If I can keep him from looking at the painting closely, I'll have no problem in convincing him.'

Mark grunted, not looking at her properly.

She found herself staring at the way the dark hair curled on the back of Mark's neck.

'You don't need to worry about Philip.'

'Don't I? That's not how it seems to

me, huge bouquets and asking you out. I couldn't help but hear; he wasn't exactly whispering. And I don't believe he's given up yet, not by a long way.'

Suddenly Lisa understood. Could Mark be jealous? A joyful warmth was spreading all through her as she took a step closer to him.

'Those expensive flowers were far too showy for me. I'd far rather have a dandelion from someone I really cared for.'

Mark's voice was quivering slightly.

'Not daisies or forget-me-nots?'

His lips were so close. It was that moorland rainstorm all over again.

Lisa said, 'I don't think so, thanks. Those have been done already.' And this kiss was every bit as overwhelming as that first one had been. She knew now that Mark had no need to be jealous of Philip, no need at all.

Philip was back within minutes and with a look of steely determination but Lisa dealt with that by making sure she got in first.

'I'm to give my mother's apologies, I'm afraid. She's had a long day.'

'I'm sorry, of course,' Philip said formally. 'But it's you I wish to see.'

Her feelings for Mark were a new discovery and this meant Lisa was viewing Philip in a different light. She almost felt sorry for him, knowing what his expectations had been. She must let him down gently, not an easy task. Lisa felt uneasily aware of all the nuances of his expression.

When she tried to usher him into the dining-room, however, he shook his head.

'I would rather talk where we can see the painting, if you wouldn't mind, as that is to be the main object of our discussion.'

Lisa's knees felt weak with relief. So his return did not involve any unwanted romantic agenda.

Philip was leading her firmly into the sitting-room and pointing accusingly at the painting.

'I must speak first, Lisa. Before you

say anything, I have to tell you that you have been the victim of an unscrupulous fraud. This is a fake.'

She stared at him. 'Yes, but we . . . '

'Very clever, and in your father's style, but I knew him so well. I have documentation listing all his paintings. There is no record of this one. It's been done very skilfully, I grant you, and I am unhappy to be causing you distress by telling you this, but it isn't fair to let you go on.'

Lisa stared at him, trying to gather her thoughts. This wasn't part of the plan. She would have to think on her feet here. But perhaps it wasn't too bad after all.

'Philip, I know,' Lisa said, smiling. 'I know all about it. And it is a genuine, unknown Carlton Clive. Honestly.'

He frowned. 'Impossible. Where has it come from?'

She took a deep breath.

'You'd better sit down.' Now she had Carol's agreement she could tell Philip everything, except the part about using

Mark's painting as a decoy. 'You didn't see the report in the local paper the other day? Last week's charity event?'

Philip shrugged. 'Oh, that. I kept away. Pamela Harris and I have never seen eye to eye. We had an unpleasant little incident with a painting I was selling, some years ago. And, no, I don't usually bother with the local paper. There's never anything in it.'

Lisa took a deep breath.

'In that case, I'll have to start from scratch.'

It was not long before any annoyance at being left out of this major portion of Carlton Clive's life was overtaken by genuine fascination on Philip's part and there was an awareness of possible self-interest in his eyes.

Philip walked over to the painting.

'Of course, I should have realised straightaway. The title and the difference in the typical trademark butterfly. Foolish of me, but I was taken completely by surprise.'

'Yes, you would be. So was I.'

She was unable to keep the sadness from her voice.

Philip turned and looked at her, picking up on her feelings at last. In one stride, he had stepped back to place his hands on her shoulders.

'This has hit you hard. What a selfish fool I am! I should have thought of that.'

Lisa thought, yes, you should. But she knew she was being unreasonable again.

'It doesn't matter.'

'But it does. You are very important to me, Lisa.'

'Yes, of course, as you are to my mother and me.' She took a deep breath. 'We have to talk about this, Philip.'

He was ignoring her.

'Oh, no, Lisa. I aim to be much more than that.'

His arms were round her like snakes and his lips were on hers.

She put her hands firmly against his chest and pushed, hard. 'I thought I'd made my feelings clear, Philip. That was not on the agenda, not at all.'

He was panting a little, his face reddening.

'You expect me to believe that? And when you have blatantly engineered being here on your own with me?'

'What else could I do? At one point I did feel that our relationship could have become closer. Now I know that it can't. The least I could do was to try and explain.' Naturally Philip must be disappointed, but she had never seen this aspect of his character before. There was no possibility of letting Philip in on their plan. Mark had been right about that.

Philip was sneering.

'I know what this is about, or whom. I had every chance until he came on the scene. Your new boyfriend is taking you for a ride. Don't think that he's interested in you for yourself. It's because you're Carlton Clive's daughter. And no doubt he's hoping the police will recover your painting and together the two works will be worth a fantastic amount.'

Lisa's hands were clenched. She unclasped them deliberately, trying to relax. She was within a hairsbreadth of losing her temper and letting go with a torrent of anger which would solve nothing. She took a deep breath.

'No, this is silly. Let's forget it ever happened and go back to where we were. Please?'

There was a moment of silence when she thought she had failed before Philip, too, was straightening his shoulders, as if mentally shaking himself.

'You're right. My fault entirely.' His voice was strained but controlled.

'I value your friendship, Philip. We always have, mother and myself. So, friends again?'

He nodded. As he turned to face her, to Lisa's relief the smiling expression was once again that of the Philip she had always known.

'I would certainly hope so. I would be very disappointed at the thought of anything other.' He paused in the doorway. 'Are you sure I cannot persuade you to at least reconsider my proposal?'

'No, I'm sorry. I won't change my mind.' Part of her was sorry but she knew beyond doubt that she was making the right decision.

'I understand. Sometimes it's difficult to make the correct decisions. But you have made your choice and we shall both have to live with that. I suppose I must feel complimented that you have confided in me.'

'Confided? Oh, about the painting.'

He nodded back towards the sitting-room.

'Of course. I certainly appreciate being allowed to share in the story of *Gemini*. This means a great deal to me.' He smiled. 'A consolation prize, you could say.'

11

They agreed that Carol, Lisa and Bobby would wait in the attic studio. That way, the house would appear exactly as it had on the night of the original theft, with only one light showing.

Each evening, Lisa had prepared the sitting-room with several footstools and waste bins placed strategically so that anyone attempting to cross the floor quietly, even with a torch, would find the process difficult. And the painting was wired much more securely than usual to its hook on the wall.

As they entered the attic room and Lisa put Bobby's basket down, however, Carol was staring round at the collection of boxes.

'I never thought to ask. Why ever were you up here that night?'

Lisa took a deep breath. What did it

matter when she knew she couldn't go through with the project, however much money it might bring in? It would be far too hurtful.

'I'm sorry. I wanted to look at Dad's papers. I know you'd said it was something I hadn't to do, and now I know why.'

Her mother gave her a hug.

'Yes, you do. I was protecting you, as I thought. Mistakenly perhaps. Well, definitely, because I couldn't have protected you for ever and it would have been much better if I'd told you myself instead of allowing you to find out.'

'Never mind. I didn't find anything here anyway. And if you had told me, what about Mark? I might have taken steps to avoid him.'

Her mother scanned her face intently.

'And that would matter, wouldn't it? Oh, I picked up on your ruse. I knew it was an excuse to enable him to guard the painting. But that doesn't matter.

There's something very worthwhile between you and Mark.' She shook her head, smiling. 'I would never have envisaged myself actually welcoming a relationship between you and Helen's son, not after so much bitterness.'

'Yes,' Lisa said softly. 'I think it's worthwhile, too. I'm so glad you can take it this way. I didn't intend falling for him; somehow my feelings for Mark have crept up on me. I think even before I knew the story, it was already too late.'

'If you and Mark can be happy together, perhaps that will be the healing process that's needed, putting everything right.' Carol's eyes filled with tears. 'Please make a success of this, Lisa, for my sake. This is the best thing that could have happened.'

Lisa swallowed. 'Don't worry, I've no intention of letting him get away.'

Her mother was hugging her again. 'Just listen to me. No-one should know better than I do how life can be filled with good intentions and equally, full of surprises, not all of them pleasant. But I do have a good instinct about you and Mark.'

She broke away, scrubbing briskly at her face with a tissue.

'We'd better snap out of this, hadn't we? Or we're not going to be a great deal of use.' She took a step back, looking closely at Lisa's face. 'Was that all there was to it or did you want to see Carlton's papers for a particular reason?'

The question took Lisa by surprise, no doubt just as her mother had intended. Lisa opened her mouth and shut it again, grasping for the phrases she had rehearsed and which would explain everything so cleverly.

Only a few moments ago, she had been on the brink of explaining the whole thing and then somehow, they had got on to her relationship with Mark.

'Were you merely seeking the truth, or was there more to it than that?' Carol Clive said quietly.

Lisa made an effort to pull herself together.

'Yes, there was and it's high time I came clean on this. I very much wanted to write a book about him, but, of course, now I see why you were always so against the very idea. It's all right, Mum. It will never happen. It's impossible. I see that now.'

Carol was nodding slowly.

'I thought it must be something like that. Oh, Lisa, you've no idea how many times I've been tempted to bring everything out into the open. And now I do believe this is the right time. A book could be a very good idea. It will be a release for all of us, and for me in particular.'

'Are you sure?' Lisa asked doubtfully. 'Don't get carried away. We've had a very emotional few days, one way or another. I wouldn't want you to make any decision you might regret later.'

'I've been mulling it over for some time now. I always came up against my supposed need to protect you. But you know, I realised last week that hanging on to the secret is going to be more trouble than releasing it. Jenny showed me that. Some of our conversations were becoming very complicated as I strove not to reveal too much. Jenny's always been very sharp, too sharp.'

'I think I noticed.'

'But you see, she has her uses. I decided I wasn't going to sit on the fence doing nothing for one moment more. You can imagine my surprise when I saw both Mark and the painting and realised that events had overtaken me.'

'But what about the publicity? It won't be too pleasant.'

'I'm sure I can take it if you can. Besides, any publicity will work in our favour. As soon as the facts are known, Mark's painting will increase in value, as will ours, of course. And if they can both arrive on the market together . . . '

'That would be wonderful. But we've to get ours back yet.'

'Oh, I'm sure we shall. Mark's plan is

excellent. Can't fail.'

Lisa smiled, sharing her mother's optimism. Yes, they had to believe that. Lisa had expected the time spent in their self-imposed imprisonment to drag by but there was now so much to do and to talk about that the time flew past.

They began again, together, in sorting through Carlton Clive's papers. From time to time, Bobby would snuffle eagerly around their feet as if wanting to join in before eventually getting bored and curling up in his basket.

It was only when her mother yawned several times that Lisa realised how late it was. She looked at her watch. Surely, if anything had been going to happen that night, it would have happened by now.

'There's just one more box, in the cupboard in the other attic,' Carol said. 'Bills mainly, I think. And after that, I shall have to give up for tonight.' She sighed. 'It doesn't look as if our lovely plan is working, does it? Perhaps it isn't so easy to predict the workings of the criminal mind and how they might react. But still, we tried. We'll just have to think of something else.'

'I'll get it,' Lisa said.

She was longer than she had anticipated as the dusty box had become stuck beneath an old desk. 'Here we are,' she called, carrying her trophy in front of her. The studio was empty. Lisa frowned.

'Mother? Where are you?'

Where could Carol be? She looked out on to the landing. No sign of her. But why hadn't Bobby made a fuss when Carol left? Surely he would have noticed? And where was Bobby? His basket was now empty.

Oh, no. Lisa opened the one of the windows and stuck her head out and sure enough, Carol was hurrying across the garden.

'Come back,' Lisa cried, fruitlessly because her mother had disappeared round the corner of the garage and couldn't possibly hear her. What could Carol be thinking of? But, of course, given the opportunity, Bobby would be making for his favourite place.

Her first thought was to follow, but that would be silly, at least without telling Mark what she was going to do. She pressed out his number on her mobile phone and explained.

'I'll go after her.'

'No, I'll go,' Mark said. 'I'm nearer. You know it makes sense.'

'Be careful.'

'Of course. I don't think anything's going to happen tonight anyway. It's later already than the first incident. When I've retrieved Carol and Bobby, I think we should call it a night. We three will still be down here with our sleeping bags.'

'That's fine.' Lisa couldn't help yawning. The house seemed completely still. They were right. Nothing would happen now, and yet she would feel happier when Carol and Bobby were safely back. She sat down again and frowned. What was that noise? Of course, it must be Mark letting himself out through the kitchen door. But it hadn't sounded like the kitchen door.

She was already reaching for her phone as it began to vibrate.

'Yes? Is that you, Mark? What's happening?'

But it was Gary, one of Mark's back-up force. His voice sounded strained.

'I'm sorry. We've made a mess of things. Keep inside the room. Lock yourself in and stay there.'

'Why? What's going on?'

'We've been locked in down here, in the cupboard under the stairs. We can't do a thing. The door won't budge.'

'Right.' She wanted to ask how on earth that had happened, but no time for that now. Her brain was moving swiftly. 'Don't worry. I'll think of something.'

'Yes, phoning the police. And we've done that already.'

'That's good. OK. 'Bye now.'

How long would they take to get here? She pressed her lips together.

Action stations, Lisa thought. It was down to her now. She wasn't intending to do anything stupid but if she could release Gary and Brian, they could get a look at the thief. A description and the car number would do, nothing more ambitious.

She didn't stop to think whether this was a good idea or not. She had to protect Mark's painting. Already, she was creeping down the first flight of stairs, not easy in the dark but easier for her than for the would-be thieves.

As she came to the last flight, there was hardly any need for quiet. Gary and Brian could be heard banging on the cupboard door. Inside the sitting-room, there were thumps and bangs as if someone was falling over the furniture. Good, Lisa thought, at least something was going as planned, and the wires that secured the painting would delay him, too — but not for long.

171

It was obvious now that the men were trying to break the under-stairs door down. Not much hope of that. Lisa knew how solid this house was. She drew in her breath at the sight of the front door, which was standing wide open, just as before.

And this time, Lisa thought triumphantly, she knew she had locked it. So it hadn't been her fault in the first place. Well, the thief wouldn't find his escape route so easily this time.

Swiftly, she hurried over and pushed the door closed, locking and bolting it, anything to gain time. She glanced at the door under the stairs but there was no sign of the key; obviously the thief had been cleverer than they had expected. No time to waste or their quarry would be escaping.

Lisa turned to the sitting-room and froze. Through the half-open door and in the faint glow of the street lights across the garden, she could see the black figure standing in front of the fireplace.

It was the same man. She was certain of that.

Her heart felt as if something had squashed it. Forgetting all caution, she was fired with a sudden anger. This villain was invading her house. Worse than that, he was taking Mark's painting. She had to stop him.

Everything was moving in slow motion. The thief still had no idea anyone was watching him as he slid the painting into a large plastic bin bag. Lisa dodged back behind the doorway as he turned, and snatched an umbrella from the hall stand. Timing . . . she had to judge this exactly. All her senses were concentrated on anticipating his footsteps and where he was.

Now! As he came through the door, she thrust the umbrella at his knees. He crumpled and went down and the painting slid across the floor. Lisa snatched at the light switch as he scrambled to his feet but again his face was hidden by a black woollen hat. As he ran for the door, Lisa ran after him.

All the possibilities were flashing through her mind at the speed of light. Yes, they had the painting but if they let him get away, there would be nothing to stop him trying again. And it wouldn't help in getting their *Gemini* back. She had to stop him and she had to find out who he was.

He was scrabbling at the bolts on the door as Lisa pulled at the black hat. He was trying to push her away but she had it. Yes! The man groaned, shoving her back with both hands, trying to keep his head down as Lisa fell on to the floor. But he was too late.

'Philip!' Lisa cried as from behind her, the kitchen door banged and Mark launched himself on to the intruder like a vengeful torpedo.

Lisa rolled away from the flailing limbs as Philip kicked out but he was no match for Mark. His arms were being twisted behind his back and Mark was sitting on him, panting.

'Lisa, are you all right?' Mark's voice was anguished.

'I'm fine,' Lisa said quickly. 'Where's the key?' she demanded, turning to Philip. He nodded to his pocket. There was hardly any need to release Gary and Brian. In the face of Mark's fury, Philip had no chance of escape. The three men pulled him to his feet and he shrugged his shoulders. He was beaten and knew it.

Mark threw his arms round Lisa.

'Are you all right? When I saw you fall . . . '

'I'm OK. It's fine, Mark, really. I slipped, that's all.'

'I told you to stay out of this. I didn't want you to get hurt.' She could feel his shoulders shaking. 'If anything had happened to you . . . '

'It didn't. And everything's turned out for the best.'

Carol Clive came in from the kitchen with Bobby in her arms.

'Philip!' Her voice was unsteady. 'Why? I valued you as a friend. You of all people, to do this to us. I can hardly believe it.'

Philip laughed harshly.

'If he hadn't appeared, sticking his nose in, I had everything planned. I was never going to keep *Gemini With Daisies*. I was going to return it to you, Carol. The whole point was to make you see that selling was your best option, to show you that keeping it here, in this insecure environment, was no longer sensible.'

'How did you get in?' Carol Clive asked.

Philip shrugged. 'That was easy. I've been here so many times that I know exactly how your security lights trigger off and how your alarm works. Borrowing a spare key and having a copy made wasn't a problem.'

'Borrowing? That was stealing, too.' Carol's voice was disgusted.

'No, it wasn't, or the painting, not when I was certain that eventually, Lisa and I would be together. It was only a matter of time.' He glared at Mark. 'You wrecked the whole thing. You've ruined my life.'

Lisa said, secure with Mark's arms around her as if he couldn't bear to let go, 'You can't plan love, Philip. I always liked you, as a friend, and at one time I agreed that the friendship might become something more.'

Yet she had made so many excuses to herself against confiding fully in Philip. She must have had a deep-seated instinct about him without realising it.

'Once I'd met Mark, I knew there could never be anything between you and me. I told you. You should have accepted that.'

'We could have grown closer. I only needed the chance.'

Lisa shook her head.

'No. No way. There's only one man in my life now. But if you hadn't stolen our painting, whatever your original motives, I would never have met Mark.' And Philip would have to live with that. He had brought all his problems upon himself.

Already the turbulent spring was blooming into a glorious summer. Mark and Lisa were snatching a few precious moments together, sitting on the garden wall, overlooking the hill and the steeply huddled houses below.

Mark put an arm round her shoulders and she sighed in contentment as she leaned against him.

'I keep going back to that night,' Mark said. 'When I thought Philip had hurt you, I knew you were more important to me than anyone or anything.' He paused. 'You said there was only one man in your life. Did you really mean that?'

'Of course I meant it,' Lisa said. 'I felt a spark of something between us the first moment I saw you, even though I was so concerned about *Gemini* at the time. I didn't recognise it until afterwards.'

Mark was so busy these days, but in the joyful and productive activity of becoming a full-time sculptor. The sale of the twin paintings had brought in an amount 'way in excess of what any of them had ever expected, more than enough to solve Carol's and Lisa's financial problems and support the charity that had been close to Helen Ridgely's heart. Lisa was overwhelmed with happiness, and she was busy, too. When the story broke, she had been approached by more than one publisher over the possibility of the book.

Her mother was humming to herself up in the attic studio at this moment and soon Lisa would go back inside up the stairs to take another turn at editing and ordering her father's papers. Prising her mother away to take the occasional break was more difficult; at last Carol Clive was allowing all the bitterness and hurt that had dogged her life to pour out.

But both women were determined, all the same, that the book should concentrate on the beauty of Carlton Clive's paintings.

'I'll have to go,' Mark said. 'I've got that appointment with the gallery in York.'

'I know.' Lisa rested her chin on his shoulder. 'Oh, Mark, I do love you.'

'And I love you.' Mark's voice was soft. 'I'm just glad that I took my paintings to the civic hall that evening. I almost didn't.'

'Don't.' Lisa shuddered. 'I don't even want to think about that. I'm so happy that everything has turned out this way.'

'I know. Strange to think that your father's legacy of pain and heartbreak has resulted in our happiness. No regrets?'

'Absolutely not. I never dreamed I could feel like this. And we owe it all to the two paintings.'

Their lips met and Lisa was singing inside. Thank you, she thought, thank you, Gemini twins.

We do hope that you have enjoyed reading this large print book.

Did you know that all of our titles are available for purchase?

We publish a wide range of high quality large print books including:
Romances, Mysteries, Classics
General Fiction
Non Fiction and Westerns

Special interest titles available in large print are:
The Little Oxford Dictionary
Music Book, Song Book
Hymn Book, Service Book

Also available from us courtesy of Oxford University Press:
Young Readers' Dictionary
(large print edition)
Young Readers' Thesaurus
(large print edition)

For further information or a free brochure, please contact us at:
Ulverscroft Large Print Books Ltd.,
The Green, Bradgate Road, Anstey,
Leicester, LE7 7FU, England.
Tel: (00 44) **0116 236 4325**
Fax: (00 44) **0116 234 0205**

THE KINDLY LIGHT

Valerie Holmes

Annie Darton's life was happiness itself, living with her father, the lighthouse keeper of Gannet Rock, until an accident changed their lives forever. Forced to move, Annie's path crosses with the attractive stranger, Zachariah Rudd. Shrouded in mystery, undoubtedly hiding something, he becomes steadily more involved in Annie's life, especially when the new lighthouse keeper is murdered. Annie finds herself drawn into the mysteries around her. Only by resolving the past can she look to the future, whatever the cost!

LOVE AND WAR

Joyce Johnson

Alison Dowland is about to marry her childhood sweetheart, Joe, when his regiment is recalled to battle, and American soldiers descend on the tiny Cornish harbour of Porthallack to prepare for the D-day landings. Excitement is high as the villagers prepare to welcome their allies, but to her dismay, Alison falls in love with American Chuck Bartlett. Amidst an agonising personal decision, she is also caught up in espionage, endangering herself and her sister.

OPPOSITES ATTRACT

Chrissie Loveday

Jeb Marlow was not happy to trust his life to the young pilot who was to fly him through a New Zealand mountain range in poor weather. What was more, the pilot was a girl. Though they were attracted, Jacquetta soon realised they lived in different worlds; he had a champagne lifestyle, dashing around the world, and she helped run an isolated fruit farm in New Zealand. Could they ever have any sort of relationship or would their differences always come between them?

WEB OF EVASION

Glenis Wilson

When Lara Denton's unmarried mother dies in a horrific horse-riding accident, she is brought up by her only relative, Grandma Emma. However, when Lara becomes a jockey, Emma disinherits her. At twenty-five, disenchanted by the male dominated world of horse racing, Lara decides to return to Bingham and make peace with Emma. Sadly, she had died. Too late, Lara realises nothing is more important than family. But who was her father? Can she unravel the mystery surrounding her birth?